Defoe Marx Hardy Abbott Montaigne Machiavelli Chesterton Cooper Emerson Joyce Austen
Melville Haggard Hugo Grimm
Stoker Christie Eliot
Carroll Molière
Wilde Maupassant Byron Schiller
Garnett Fitzgerald Engels Smith Kafka
Goethe Einstein Hawthorne Hall
Cotton Dostoyevsky Willis
Baum Henry Kipling Doyle
Leslie Dumas Flaubert Turgenev Nietzsche Balzac
Stockton Vatsyayana Crane
Burroughs Verne
Curtis Tocqueville Gogol Vinci
Homer Widger Tolstoy Whitman Busch
Darwin Thoreau Twain Scott Harte
Potter Freud Zola Lawrence Plato
Kant Jowett Stevenson Dickens Hesse
Andersen Burton
London Descartes Cervantes
Poe Aristotle Wells Voltaire Cooke
Hale James Hastings Irving
Bunner Shakespeare Chambers
Richter Chekhov da Shaw Benedict Alcott
Doré Dante Swift Pushkin
Newton Wodehouse

The Gamester (1753)

Edward Moore

Imprint

This book is part of TREDITION CLASSICS

Author: Edward Moore
Cover design: Buchgut, Berlin – Germany

Publisher: tredition GmbH, Hamburg - Germany
ISBN: 978-3-8424-8089-6

www.tredition.com
www.tredition.de

CONTENTS

INTRODUCTION

This reprint of Edward Moore's TheGamester makes available to students of eighteenth century literature a play which, whatever its intrinsic merits, is historically important both as a vehicle for a century of great actors and as a contribution to the development of middle-class tragedy which had considerable influence on the Continent. TheGamester was first presented at the Drury Lane Theatre February 7, 1753 with Garrick in the leading role, and ran for ten successive nights. Up to the middle of the nineteenth century it remained a popular stock piece--John Philip Kemble, Mrs. Siddons, Mrs. Barry, the Keans, Macready, and others having distinguished themselves in it-- and in America from 1754 to 1875 it enjoyed even more performances than in England. (J.H. Caskey, TheLifeandWorksofEdwardMoore, 96-99). Moore's middle-class tragedy is the only really successful attempt to follow Lillo's decisive break with tradition in England in the eight-eenth century. His background, like Lillo's, was humble, religious, and mercantile. The son of a dissenting pastor, Moore received his early education in dissenters' academies, and then served an apprentice-ship to a London linen-draper. After a few years in Ireland as an agent for a merchant, Moore returned to London to join a partnership in the linen trade. The partnership was soon dissolved, and Moore turned to letters for a livelihood. Among his works are FablesfortheFemaleSex (1744) which went through three editions, TheFoundling (1748), a successful comedy, and GilBlas (1751), an unsuccessful comedy. In 1753, with encouragement and some assistance from Garrick, he pro-duced TheGamester, upon which his reputation as a writer depends.

It is impossible, of course, to review here all the factors involved in the development of middle-class tragedy in England in the eighteenth century. However, certain aspects of that movement which concern Moore's immediate predecessors and which have not been adequate-ly recognized might be mentioned briefly. Aside from Elizabethan and Jacobean attempts to give tragic expression 2 to everyday human experience, historians have noted the efforts of Otway, Southerne, and Rowe to lower the social level of tragedy; but in this period mid-dle-class problems and sentiments and domestic situations appear in numerous tragedies, long-since forgotten, which in form, setting, and social level present no startling deviations from traditional standards. Little or no attention has been given to some of these obscure dramatists who in the midst of the Collier controversy attempted to illustrate in tragedy the arguments advanced in the third part of John Dennis's <u>TheUsefulnessoftheStage, totheHappinessofMankind, toGovernment, andtoReligion</u> (1698). Striving to demonstrate the usefulness of the stage, these avowed reformers produced essentially domestic tragedies, by treating such problems as filial obedience and marital fidelity in terms of orthodox theology. The argument that the stage can be an adjunct of the pulpit is widespread, and appears most explicitly in Hill's preface to his <u>FatalExtravagance</u> (1721), sometimes regarded as the first middle-class tragedy in the eighteenth century, and in Lillo's dedication to <u>GeorgeBarnwell</u> (1731). The line from these obscure dramatists at the turn of the century to Lillo is direct and clear. Of these forgotten plays we can note here only <u>FatalFriendship</u> (1698) by Mrs. Catherine Trotter whom John Hughes hailed as "the first of stage-reformers"

(<u>TotheAuthorofFatalFriendship, aTragedy</u>), an unquestionably domestic tragedy inculcating a theological "lesson". To this play, which was acted with "great applause" (<u>BiographicaDramatica</u>, 107), Aaron Hill was, I am convinced, considerably indebted for his <u>FatalExtravagance</u>, which is, in turn, one of the sources of <u>TheGamester</u>.

In the early eighteenth century, then, there is clearly discernible a two-fold tendency toward middle-class tragedy which reaches its fullest expression in Lillo: the desire to lower the social level of the characters in order to make the tragedy more moving; and the desire to defend the stage by demonstrating its religious and moral utility. In his prologue to <u>TheFairPenitent</u> (1703), Rowe gave expression to the first: the "fate of kings and empires", he argues, 3 is too remote to engage our feelings, for "we ne'er can pity that we ne'er can share"; therefore he offers "a melancholy tale of private woes". In his prologue, Lillo repeats this idea, but in his dedication he shows himself primarily concerned with the second tendency. Specifically challenging those "who deny the lawfulness of the stage", he argues that "the more extensively useful the moral of any tragedy is, the more excellent that piece must be of its kind"; the generality of mankind is more liable to vice than are kings; therefore "plays founded on moral tales in private life may be of admirable use... by stifling vice in its first principles". Dramatists who were concerned only or primarily with the first of these tendencies (the emotional effect), produced domestic or pseudo-domestic tragedies in the manner of Otway and Rowe. But those who stressed the second (moral and religious utility), seeking practical themes of widespread applicability, quite logically moved toward genuine middle-class tragedy. Thus Hill's <u>FatalExtravagance</u> is concerned with the "vice" of gambling; while Charles Johnson's <u>Caelia</u>, <u>orThePerjur'd Lover</u> (1732) attacks fashionable libertinism of the day, telling the story which Richardson was later to retell in seven ponderous volumes. In <u>Caelia</u> the religious rationalization of the tragic action is subdued, Johnson apparently preferring to stress the social and moral aspects of his subject, and to this end he resolutely refused to expunge or modify the boldly realistic brothel scenes, against which a fastidious audience had protested.

A comparison of <u>TheGamester</u> with its predecessor, <u>FatalExtravagance</u>, reflects certain developments in the intellectual background of the first half of the eighteenth century. Hill anticipated Lillo in repeating Rowe's argument for lowering the social level of tragedy and in stating vigorously his desire to defend the stage by demonstrating its religious and moral utility. An admirer of Dennis's critical writings, Hill repeats Dennis's argument that the stage can affect those whom the pulpit falls to reach, and he offers his play

as proof that "sound and useful instruction may be drawn from the <u>Theatre</u>", challenging the enemies of the stage to test his play "by the rules of religion 4 and virtue" (Preface). Taking a "hint", as he says, from <u>AYorkshireTragedy</u>, Hill endeavored to show the "private sorrows" that result from gaming.

At the opening of the play, the hero, having gambled away his fortune, faces poverty. His friend who signed his bond is in jail and a kindly uncle has failed to secure the needed relief. In a fit of passion growing out of despair, the hero kills the villainous creditor, and decides to poison his (the hero's) wife and children, and then stab himself. In his dying moments he learns that the uncle has substituted a harmless cordial for the poison and that a long-lost brother has died leaving him a fortune. This bare outline gives no indication of Hill's careful theological rationalization of character and plot which he promised in his preface. Hill incorporated in his play the teachings of orthodox divines; there is nothing 'revolutionary' in his analytical presentation of human nature. The theological significance of Hill's play has not, to my knowledge, been recognized; thematic passages tend to be dismissed as tiresome and gratuitous moralizing and the plot is often regarded as empty melodrama or the representation of some ambiguous 'fate'. It is in this deliberate theological rationalization of his materials that Hill owes most to Mrs. Trotter's domestic tragedy and that he differs significantly from Moore.

As with Hill and Lillo, Moore's desire to write a play with an extensively useful 'moral' led him to middle-class realism and prose. To attack the widespread fashion of gaming which he regarded as a "vice", Moore attempted to present "a natural picture" in language adapted "to the capacities and feelings of every part of the audience" (Preface, 1756). That he should have treated this social problem tragically is to be explained, perhaps, by his sources and by his religious background. He justified the "horror of its catastrophe" on the grounds that "so prevailing and destructive a vice as Gaming" warranted it. <u>TheGamester</u> has been justly credited with superior dramatic qualities in comparison with Hill's <u>FatalExtravagance,</u>, but we might perhaps note briefly certain aspects of the two plays which reflect changes in the intellectual background. In both plays theological ideas are involved in the treatment of the fall of the hero, partially 5 in Moore's play, completely In Hill's. Not recognizing ideas common to early eighteenth century sermons, the modern reader may perhaps puzzle over the steadily increasing moral paralysis and despondency in Moore's hero, <u>Beverly</u>. Vice, preached the divines, beclouds the reason, leaving it progressively incapable of controlling the passions:

Follies, if uncontroul'd, of every kind,
Grow into passions, and subdue the mind. (V, 4)

Further each commission of sin causes progressive loss of grace, without which man cannot act rightly. In prison <u>Beverly</u> is incapable of prayer ("I cannot pray--Despair has laid his iron hand upon me, and seal'd me for perdition..."). However, a benevolent deity touches him with the finger of grace, enabling him to repent ("I wish'd for ease, a moment's ease, that cool repentance and contrition might soften vengeance"). He can now pray for mercy and in his dying moments is vouchsafed assurance of forgiveness ("Yet Heaven is gracious--I ask'd for hope, as the bright presage of forgiveness, and like a light, blazing thro' darkness, it came and chear'd me...").

In this aspect Moore is working along the lines laid down by Hill, but there is a significant difference, attributable perhaps to the weakening of orthodox theology and the spreading influence of the Shaftesburian school of ethical theorists. In the older theology, man's progressive loss of grace correspondingly releases his natural propensity for evil, and working in these concepts neither Hill nor Lillo hesitated to show his hero descending to murder. Moore, influenced perhaps by the ethical sentiments of the day, compromised his theological concepts and permitted his hero no really evil act (excluding of course his suicide), and stressed instead Beverly's mistaken trust in Stukely, who is, as Elton has pointed out, a "Mandevillian man" (SurveyofEnglishLiterature:1730-1760, I, 329-30).

There is another significant difference between the two plays which reflects the development of religious thought in the first half of the eighteenth century. Commenting on the too-late arrival of the news of the uncle's death, 6 Elton remarks that "this too-lateness... which is in the nature of an accident, is a common and mechanical device of Georgian tragedy" (I, 330). Hill employed the device, the good news coming as a complete surprise, but he made it part of a carefully ordered plot designed to reveal the direct intervention and mysterious workings of a particular Providence, making characterization and action consistent, and giving his play a precise theological significance. In Moore's day, however, under the impact of deism and the developing rationalism, the concept of a particular Providence in orthodox theology had become so subtilized that the older idea of direct and striking intervention in human affairs all but disappeared. By mid-eighteenth century, deity, as Leslie Stephen points out, "appears under the colourless shape of Providence--a word which may be taken to imply a remote divine superintendence, without admitting an actual divine interference" (HistoryofEnglishThoughtIntheEighteenthCentury, II, 336). The references to Providence in Moore's play are of this type, pious labels on prudential morality. Moore carefully avoids the various devices employed by Hill to indicate direct divine intervention; consequently the late arrival of the news of the uncle's death (which was expected throughout the play) is without special meaning, and serves only as a theatrical device intended to heighten the emotional effect. <u>TheGamester</u>, then, is a clear reflection of the state of English thought in the middle of the eighteenth century, in which a declining theology becomes suffused with the ideas and sentiments of the moralists of the age.

Despite the popularity of their plays, neither Lillo nor Moore inspired any significant followers in England. On the Continent, however, their influence was considerable. In his introduction to his edition of <u>TheLondonMerchant</u>, A.W. Ward traces Lillo's influence on the Continent, and Caskey gives a detailed account of Moore's (119-134). <u>TheGamester</u> was translated into German, French, Dutch, Spanish, and Italian. It was first acted at Breslau in 1754 and retained its stage popularity for more than two decades. A German translation appeared in 1754, and for more than twenty years numerous editions and translations 7 continued to appear. In France, Diderot admired the play and translated it in 1760 (not published until 1819); Saurin's translation and adaptation (1767) proved popular on the French stage (he later provided an alternate happy ending which was frequently played).

<u>TheGamester</u> is reproduced, with permission, from a copy owned by the University of Michigan.

Charles H. Peake

University of Michigan

1

BIBLIOGRAPHICAL NOTE

The first edition of Moore's <u>TheGamester</u> appeared in 1753 shortly after the opening of Garrick's performance of the play on February 7. This edition is in many respects a good text; it has seemed desirable for several reasons, however, to reprint this work from the 1756 edition of <u>Poems</u>, <u>Fables</u>, <u>andPlays</u> (often referred to as the "Collected

Works"). The 1756 text often corrects that of 1753 and is generally superior to later printings; it contains passages and improved readings not present in other editions; it aims at formal correctness, employing classical scene division; as a "Works" edition it exhibits excellent editorial and typographical treatment; it enjoys a superior general readability advantageous to classroom use; and, finally, it contains Moore's vindicatory preface, which, as far as an examination of available copies shows, does not appear in other editions. Inasmuch as the 1756 printing is somewhat late, standing between the fourth and fifth editions of the play, a brief bibliographical account of TheGamester is offered.

The play was printed separately many times in the eighteenth century. The first edition, in the University of Michigan copy, bears the title: THE / GAMESTER. / A / TRAGEDY. / As it is Acted at the / Theatre-Royal in Drury-Lane. / [rule] / ornament / [rule] / LONDON: / Printed for R. FRANCKLIN, in Russel-Street, / Covent-Garden; and Sold by R. DODSLEY, / in Pall-Mall. M.DCC.LIII. / The anonymity of the titlepage is half-hearted, for the dedication to Henry Pelham is signed "Edw. Moore." A prologue written by Garrick, an epilogue, and the cast of the original performance precede the eighty-four page text. Francklin and Dodsley brought out a second edition in the same year and a fourth edition in 1755; presumably a third edition had been issued in the interim. In 1771 a fifth and a sixth edition appeared, and in 1776 another London edition came out. In 1784 two more editions made an appearance, the first printed for R. Butters (John H. Caskey, TheLifeandWorksofEdwardMoore, Yale Studies in English, LXXV [New Haven, 1927], p. 174), the second 2 printed for a group of four booksellers--Thomas Davies, W. Nicoll, Samuel Bladon, and John Bew. The same combination of booksellers, with W. Lowndes taking the place of Davies, issued in 1789 an inferior reprinting of their 1784 text. The editions of 1784 and 1789 are interesting because they identify by inverted commas the cuts made in contemporary stage versions. Before the end of the century three editions were printed outside London: two Dublin imprints of 1763 and 1783, and an American imprint of 1791 by Henry Taylor in Philadelphia.

In addition to these separate publications, TheGamester was included in two collections of Moore's works. The 1756 edition has already been noticed. THE DRAMATIC WORKS OF Mr. Edward Moore, as the 1788 titlepage describes the volume, was issued by the Lowndes-Nicoll-Bladon-Bew group and was actually an assembled text made up of the 1784 printing of <u>TheGamester</u>, the 1786 <u>TheFoundling</u>, and the 1788 <u>GilBlas</u>.

The play was a favorite in many popular dramatic collections of the late eighteenth and early nineteenth century; it appeared in Bell's <u>BritishTheatre</u> in 1776 and thereafter, in Mrs. Inchbald's <u>TheBritishTheatre</u> in 1808, in Dibdin's <u>LondonTheatre</u> in 1815, and in Cumberland's <u>BritishTheatre</u> in 1826. According to Caskey and other sources the play was thus reprinted more than a dozen times by the middle of the nineteenth century. Since then it has declined in favor and has seldom been reprinted, even in textbook anthologies covering representative literature of the period.

The 1756 text of the play and the plates from the Davies-Nicoll-Bladon-Bew 1784 edition have been reproduced through the cooperation of the University of Michigan Library from copies of these editions in its possession. Because of its lack of significance, the dedication to Henry Pelham has not been reprinted.

Philip R. Wikelund

University of Michigan

THE

GAMESTER.

A

TRAGEDY.

As it is Acted at the

THEATRE-ROYAL

IN

DRURY-LANE.

GAMESTER.

Mrs. SIDDONS and Mr. KEMBLE as
Mr. & Mrs. Beverley Act 5. Sc. 4.

*Bev. O! for a few short Moments to tell you how my
Heart bleeds for you.*

417Hhh

PREFACE.

It having been objected to this tragedy, that its language is prose, and its catastrophe too horrible, I shall entreat the reader's patience for a minute, that I may say a word or two to these objections.

The play of the GAMESTER *was intended to be a natural picture of that kind of life, of which all men are judges; and as it struck at a vice so universally prevailing, it was thought proper to adapt its language to the capacities and feelings of every part of the audience: that as some of its characters were of no higher rank than* Sharpers, *it was imagined that (whatever good company they may find admittance to in the world) their speaking blank verse upon the stage would be unnatural, if not ridiculous. But though the more elevated characters also speak prose, the judicious reader will observe, that it is a species of prose which differs very little from verse: in many of the most animated scenes, I can truly say, that I often found it a much greater difficulty to avoid, 418 than to write,* measure. *I shall only add, in answer to this objection, that I hoped to be more interesting, by being more natural; and the event, as far as I have been a witness of it, has more than answered my expectations.*

As to the other objection, the horror of its catastrophe, if it be considered simply what that catastrophe is, and compared with those of other tragedies, I should humbly presume that the working it up to any uncommon degree of horror, is the merit *of the play, and not its* reproach. *Nor should so prevailing and destructive a vice as* GAMING *be attacked upon the theatre, without impressing upon the imagination all the horrors that may attend it.*

I shall detain the reader no longer than to inform him, that I am indebted for many of the most popular passages in this play to the inimitable performer, who, in the character of the Gamester, *exceeded every idea I had conceived of it in the writing.*

PROLOGUE.

Written and spoken by Mr. GARRICK.

Like fam'd La Mancha's knight, who launce in hand,
Mounted his steed to free th' enchanted land,
Our Quixote bard sets forth a monster-taming,
Arm'd at all points, to fight that hydra — GAMING.
Aloft on Pegasus he waves his pen,
And hurls defiance at the caitiff's den.
The First on fancy'd giants spent his rage,
But This has more than windmills to engage:
He combats passion, rooted in the soul,
Whose pow'rs, at once delight ye, and controul;
Whose magic bondage each lost slave enjoys,
Nor wishes freedom, though the spell destroys.
To save our land from this MAGICIAN's charms,
And rescue maids and matrons from his arms,
Our knight poetic comes. And Oh! ye fair!
This black ENCHANTER's wicked arts beware!
His subtle poison dims the brightest eyes,
And at his touch, each grace and beauty dies:
Love, gentleness and joy to rage give way,
And the soft dove becomes a bird of prey.
May this our bold advent'rer break the spell,
And drive the demon to his native hell.
* Ye slaves of passion, and ye dupes of chance,*
Wake all your pow'rs from this destructive trance!
Shake off the shackles of this tyrant vice:
Hear other calls than those of cards and dice:
Be learn'd in nobler arts, than arts of play,
And other debts, than those of honour pay:
No longer live insensible to shame,
Lost to your country, families and fame.
* Could our romantic muse this work atchieve,*
Would there one honest heart in Britain grieve?
Th' attempt, though wild, would not in vain be made,
If every honest hand would lend its aid.

Dramatis Personae.

MEN.

Beverley,	Mr. GARRICK.
Lewson,	Mr. MOSSOP.
Stukely,	Mr. DAVIES.
Jarvis,	Mr. BERRY.
Bates,	Mr. BURTON.
Dawson,	Mr. BLAKES.
Waiter,	Mr. ACKMAN.

WOMEN.

Mrs. Beverley,	Mrs. PRITCHARD.
Charlotte,	Miss. HAUGHTON.
Lucy,	Mrs. PRICE.

SCENE, LONDON.

THE

GAMESTER.

A

TRAGEDY.

ACT I. SCENE I.

Enter Mrs. Beverley, and Charlotte.

Mrs. BEVERLEY.

BE comforted, my dear; all may be well yet. And now, methinks, the lodgings begin to look with another face. O sister! sister! if these were all my hardships; if all I had to complain of were no more than quitting my house, servants, equipage and show, your pity would be weakness.

Char. Is poverty nothing then?

Mrs. Bev. Nothing in the world, if it affected only Me. While we had a fortune, I was the happiest of the rich: and now 'tis gone, give me but a bare subsistance, and my 422 husband's smiles, and I'll be the happiest of the poor. To Me now these lodgings want nothing but their master. Why d'you look so at me?

Char. That I may hate my brother.

Mrs. Bev. Don't talk so, Charlotte.

Char. Has he not undone you? Oh! this pernicious vice of gaming! But methinks his usual hours of four or five in the morning might have contented him; 'twas misery enough to wake for him till then: need he have staid out all night? I shall learn to detest him.

Mrs. Bev. Not for the first fault. He never slept from me before.

Char. Slept from you! No, no; his nights have nothing to do with sleep. How has this one vice driven him from every virtue! nay, from his affections too! — The time *was*, sister —

Mrs. Bev. And *is.* I have no fear of his affections. Would I knew that he were safe!

Char. From ruin and his companions. But that's impossible. His poor little boy too! What must become of Him?

Mrs. Bev. Why, want shall teach him industry. From his father's mistakes he shall learn prudence, and from his mother's resignation, patience. Poverty has no such terrors in it as you imagine. There's no condition of life, sickness and pain excepted, where happiness is excluded. The needy peasant, who rises early to his labour, enjoys more welcome rest at night for't. His bread is sweeter to him; his home happier; his family dearer; his enjoyments surer. The sun that rouses him in the morning, sets in the evening to release him. All situations have their comforts, if sweet contentment dwell in the heart. But my poor Beverley has none. The thought of having ruined those he loves, is misery for ever to him. Would I could ease his mind of That!

423

Char. If He alone were ruined, 'twere just he should be punished. He is my brother, 'tis true; but when I think of what he has done; of the fortune You brought him; of his own large estate too, squandered away upon this vilest of passions, and among the vilest of wretches! O! I have no patience! My own little fortune is untouched, he says: would I were sure on't!

Mrs. Bev. And so you may; 'twould be a sin to doubt it.

Char. I will be sure on't. 'Twas madness in me to give it to his management. But I'll demand it from him this morning. I have a melancholy occasion for't.

Mrs. Bev. What occasion?

Char. To support a sister.

Mrs. Bev. No; I have no need on't. Take it, and reward a lover with it. The generous Lewson deserves much more. Why won't you make him happy?

Char. Because my sister's miserable.

Mrs. Bev. You must not think so. I have my jewels left yet. I'll sell them to supply our wants; and when all's gone these hands shall toil for our support. The poor should be industrious—Why those tears, Charlotte?

Char. They flow in pity for you.

Mrs. Bev. All may be well yet. When he has nothing to lose, I shall fetter him in these arms again; and then what is it to be poor?

Char. Cure him but of this destructive passion, and my uncle's death may retrieve all yet.

Mrs. Bev. Ay, Charlotte, *could* we cure him. But the disease of play admits no cure but poverty; and the loss of another fortune would but encrease his shame and his affliction. Will Mr. Lewson call this morning?

424

Char. He said so last night. He gave me hints too, that he had suspicions of our friend Stukely.

Mrs. Bev. Not of treachery to your Brother? That he loves play I know; but surely he is honest.

Char. He would fain be thought so; therefore I doubt him. Honesty needs no pains to set itself off.

Mrs. Bev. What now, Lucy?

SCENE II.

Enter Lucy.

Lucy. Your old steward, madam. I had not the heart to deny him admittance, the good old man begged so hard for it.

[*Exit.*

SCENE III.

Enter Jarvis.

Mrs. Bev. Is this well, Jarvis? I desired you to avoid me.

Jar. Did you, madam? I am an old man, and had forgot. Perhaps too you forbad my tears; but I am old, madam, and age will be forgetful.

Mrs. Bev. The faithful creature! how he moves me!

[*To Charlotte.*

Char. Not to have seen him had been cruelty.

Jar. I have forgot these apartments too. I remember none such in my young master's house; and yet I have lived in't these five and twenty years. His good father would not have dismissed me.

Mrs. Bev. He had no reason, Jarvis.

Jar. I was faithful to him while he lived, and when he 425Iii died, he bequeathed me to his son. I have been faithful to Him too.

Mrs. Bev. I know it, I know it, Jarvis.

Char. We both know it.

Jar. I am an old man, madam, and have not a long time to live. I asked but to have died with him, and he dismissed me.

Mrs. Bev. Prithee no more of this! 'Twas his poverty that dismissed you.

Jar. Is he indeed so poor then? Oh! he was the joy of my old heart. But must his creditors have all? And have they sold his house too? His father built it when He was but a prating boy. The times I have carried him in these arms! And, Jarvis, says he, when a beggar has asked charity of me, why should people be poor? You shan't be poor, Jarvis; if I was a king, nobody should be poor. Yet He is poor. And then he was so brave!—O, he was a brave little boy! And yet so merciful, he'd not have killed the gnat that stung him.

Mrs. Bev. Speak to him, Charlotte; for I cannot.

Char. When I have wiped my eyes.

Jar. I have a little money, madam; it might have been more, but I have loved the poor. All that I have is yours.

Mrs. Bev. No, Jarvis; we have enough yet. I thank you though, and will deserve your goodness.

Jar. But shall I see my master? And will he let me attend him in his distresses? I'll be no expence to him: and 'twill kill me to be refused. Where is he, madam?

Mrs. Bev. Not at home, Jarvis. You shall see him another time.

Char. To-morrow, or the next day. O, Jarvis! what a change is here!

426

Jar. A change indeed, madam! My old heart akes at it. And yet methinks — But here's somebody coming.

SCENE IV.

Enter Lucy with Stukely.

Lucy. Mr. Stukely, Madam.

[*Exit.*

Stu. Good morning to you, Ladies. Mr. Jarvis, your servant. Where's my friend, madam?

[*To Mrs. Beverley.*

Mrs. Bev. I should have asked that question of You. Have not you seen him to-day?

Stu. No, madam.

Char. Nor last night?

Stu. Last night! Did not he come home then?

Mrs. Bev. No. Were not you together?

Stu. At the beginning of the evening; but not since. Where can he have staid?

Char. You call yourself his friend, Sir; why do you encourage him in this madness of gaming?

Stu. You have asked me that question before, madam; and I told you my concern was that I could not save him. Mr. Beverley is a man, madam; and if the most friendly entreaties have no effect upon him, I have no other means. My purse has been his, even to the injury of my fortune. If That has been encouragement, I deserve censure; but I meant it to retrieve him.

Mrs. Bev. I don't doubt it, Sir; and I thank you. But where did you leave him last night?

Stu. At Wilson's, madam, if I ought to tell; in company I did not like. Possibly he may be there still. Mr. Jarvis knows the house, I believe.

Jar. Shall I go, madam?

427Iii2

Mrs. Bev. No; he may take it ill.

Char. He may go as from himself.

Stu. And if he pleases, madam, without naming Me. I am faulty myself, and should conceal the errors of a friend. But I can refuse nothing here.

[*Bowing to the ladies.*

Jar. I would fain see him, methinks.

Mrs. Bev. Do so then. But take care how you upbraid him. I have never upbraided him.

Jar. Would I could bring him comfort!

[*Exit.*

Stu. Don't be too much alarmed, madam. All men have their errors, and their times of seeing them. Perhaps my friend's time is not come yet. But he has an uncle; and old men don't live for ever. You should look forward, madam: we are taught how to value a second fortune by the loss of a first.

[*A knocking at the door.*

Mrs. Bev. Hark!—No; that knocking was too rude for Mr. Beverley. Pray heaven he be well!

Stu. Never doubt it, madam. You shall be well too: every thing shall be well.

[*Knocking again.*

Mrs. Bev. The knocking is a little loud though. Who waits there? Will none of you answer? — None of you, did I say? Alas! I thought myself in my own house, surrounded with servants.

Char. I'll go, sister — But don't be alarmed so.

[*Exit.*

Stu. What extraordinary accident have you to fear, madam?

Mrs. Bev. I beg your pardon; but 'tis ever thus with me in Mr. Beverley's absence. No one knocks at the door, but I fancy 'tis a messenger of ill news.

Stu. You are too fearful, madam; 'twas but one night of absence; and if ill thoughts intrude (as love is always 428 doubtful) think of your worth and beauty, and drive them from your breast.

Mrs. Bev. What thoughts? I have no thoughts that wrong my husband.

Stu. Such thoughts indeed would wrong him. The world is full of slander; and every wretch that knows himself unjust, charges his neighbour with like passions; and by the general frailty, hides his own. If you are wise, and would be happy, turn a deaf ear to such reports: 'tis ruin to believe them.

Mrs. Bev. Ay, worse than ruin. 'Twould be to sin against conviction. Why was it mentioned?

Stu. To guard you against rumour. The sport of half mankind is mischief; and for a single error they make men devils. If their tales reach you, disbelieve them.

Mrs. Bev. What tales? By whom? Why told? I have heard nothing; or if I had, with all his errors, my Beverley's firm faith admits no doubt. It is my safety; my seat of rest and joy, while the storm threatens round me. I'll not forsake it. (*Stukely sighs, and looks down*) Why turn you from me? And why that sigh?

Stu. I was attentive, madam; and sighs will come we know not why. Perhaps I have been too busy. If it should seem so, impute my zeal to friendship, that meant to guard you against evil tongues. Your Beverley is wronged; slandered most vilely. My life upon his truth.

Mrs. Bev. And mine too. Who is't that doubts it? But no matter — I am prepared, Sir. — Yet why this caution? — You are my husband's friend; I think you mine too; the common friend of both. (*Pauses*) I had been unconcerned else.

429

Stu. For heaven's sake, madam, be so still! I meant to guard you *against* suspicion, not to alarm it.

Mrs. Bev. Nor have you, Sir. Who told you of suspicion? I have a heart it cannot reach.

Stu. Then I am happy — I would say more, but am prevented.

SCENE V.

Re-enter Charlotte.

Mrs. Bev. Who was it, Charlotte?

Char. What a heart has that Jarvis! — A creditor, sister. But the good old man has taken him away. Don't distress his wife! Don't distress his sister! I could hear him say. 'Tis cruel to distress the afflicted. And when he saw me at the door, he begged pardon that his friend had knocked so loud.

Stu. I wish I had known of this. Was it a large demand, madam?

Char. I heard not that; but visits such as these, we must expect often. Why so distressed, sister? This is no new affliction.

Mrs. Bev. No, Charlotte; but I am faint with watching;

quite sunk and spiritless. Will you excuse me, Sir? I'll to my chamber, and try to rest a little.

Stu. Good thoughts go with you, madam.

[*Exit Mrs. Beverley.*

My bait is taken then. (*Aside.*) Poor Mrs. Beverley! How my heart grieves to see her thus!

Char. Cure her, and be a friend then.

Stu. How cure her, madam?

Char. Reclaim my brother.

Stu. Ay; give him a new creation; or breathe another soul into him. I'll think on't, madam. Advice, I see, is thankless.

Char. Useless I am sure it is, if through mistaken friendship, or other motives, you feed his passion with your purse, and sooth it by example. Physicians, to cure fevers, keep from the patient's thirsty lip the cup that would inflame him; You give it to his hands. (*A knocking.*) Hark, Sir! These are my brother's desperate symptoms. Another creditor.

Stu. One not so easily got rid of — What, Lewson!

SCENE VI.

Enter Lewson.

Lew. Madam, your servant. Yours, Sir. I was enquiring for you at your lodgings.

Stu. This morning? You had business then?

Lew. You'll call it by another name, perhaps. Where's Mr. Beverley, madam?

Char. We have sent to enquire for him.

Lew. Is he abroad then? He did not use to go out so early.

Char. No; nor to stay out so late.

Lew. Is that the case? I am sorry for it. But Mr. Stukely, perhaps, may direct you to him.

Stu. I have already, Sir. But what was your business with Me?

Lew. To congratulate you upon your late successes at play. Poor Beverley! But You are his friend; and there's a comfort in having successful friends.

Stu. And what am I to understand by this?

Lew. That Beverley's a poor man, with a rich friend; that's all.

Stu. Your words would mean something, I suppose. Another time, Sir, I shall desire an explanation.

Lew. And why not now? I am no dealer in long sentences. A minute or two will do for me.

Stu. But not for Me, Sir. I am slow of apprehension, and must have time and privacy. A lady's presence engages my attention. Another morning I may be found at home.

Lew. Another morning then, I'll wait upon you.

Stu. I shall expect you, Sir. Madam, your servant.

[*Exit.*

Char. What mean you by this?

Lew. To hint to him that I know him.

Char. How know him? Mere doubt and supposition!

Lew. I shall have proof soon.

Char. And what then? Would you risk your life to be his punisher?

Lew. My life, madam! Don't be afraid. And yet I am happy in your concern for me. But let it content you that I know this Stukely. 'Twould be as easy to make him honest as brave.

Char. And what d'you intend to do?

Lew. Nothing, till I have proof. Yet my suspicions are well-grounded. But methinks, madam, I am acting here without authority. Could I have leave to call Mr. Beverley brother, his concerns would be my own. Why will you make my services appear officious?

Char. You know my reasons, and should not press me. But I am cold, you say: and cold I will be, while a poor sister's destitute. My heart bleeds for her! and till I see her sorrows moderated, love has no joys for me. 432*Lew.* Can I be less a friend by being a brother? I would not say an unkind thing; but the pillar of your house is shaken. Prop it with another, and it shall stand firm again. You must comply.

Char. And will, when I have peace within myself. But let us change the subject. Your business here this morning is with my sister. Misfortunes press too hard upon her: yet till to day she has borne them nobly.

Lew. Where is she?

Char. Gone to her chamber. Her spirits failed her.

Lew. I hear her coming. Let what has passed with Stukely be a secret. She has already too much to trouble her.

SCENE VII.

Enter Mrs. Beverley.

Mrs. Bev. Good morning, Sir. I heard your voice, and, as I thought, enquiring for me. Where's Mr. Stukely, Charlotte?

Char. This moment gone. You have been in tears, sister; but here's a friend shall comfort you.

Lew. Or if I add to your distresses, I'll beg your pardon, madam. The sale of your house and furniture was finished yesterday.

Mrs. Bev. I know it, Sir. I know too your generous reason for putting me in mind of it. But you have obliged me too much already.

Lew. There are trifles, madam, which you have set a value on: those I have purchased, and will deliver. I have a friend too that esteems you; he has bought largely, and will call nothing his, till he has seen you. If a visit to him would not be painful, he has begged it may be this morning.

433Kkk

Mrs. Bev. Not painful in the least. My pain is from the kindness of my friends. Why am I to be obliged beyond the power of return?

Lew. You shall repay us at your own time. I have a coach waiting at the door. Shall we have Your company, madam?

[*To Charlotte.*

Char. No. My brother may return soon; I'll stay and receive him.

Mrs. Bev. He may want a comforter, perhaps. But don't upbraid him, Charlotte. We shan't be absent long. Come, Sir, since I *must* be so obliged.

Lew. 'Tis I that am obliged. An hour or less will be sufficient for us. We shall find you at home, madam? (*To Charlotte.*)

[*Exit with Mrs. Beverley.*

Char. Certainly. I have but little inclination to appear abroad. O! this brother! this brother! to what wretchedness has he reduced us!

[*Exit.*

SCENE VIII. Changes to Stukely's lodgings.

Enter Stukely.

Stu. That Lewson suspects me, 'tis too plain. Yet why should he suspect me? I appear the friend of Beverley as well as he. But I am rich it seems: and so I am; thanks to another's folly and my own wisdom. To what use is wisdom, but to take advantage of the weak? This Beverley's my fool: I cheat him, and he calls me friend. But more business must be done yet. His wife's jewels are unsold; so is the reversion of his uncle's estate. I must have these too. And then there's a treasure above all. I love his wife. Before she knew this Beverley, I loved her; but like 434 a cringing fool, bowed at a distance, while He stept in and won her. Never, never will I forgive him for it. My pride, as well as love, is wounded by this conquest. I must have vengeance. Those hints, this morning, were well thrown in. Already they have fastened on her. If jealousy should weaken her affections, want may corrupt her virtue. My hate rejoyces in the hope. These jewels may do much. He shall demand them of her; which, when mine, shall be converted to special purposes.—What now, Bates?

SCENE IX.

Enter Bates.

Bates. Is it a wonder then to see me? The forces are in readiness, and only wait for orders. Where's Beverley?

Stu. At last night's rendezvous, waiting for Me. Is Dawson with you?

Bates. Dressed like a nobleman; with money in his pocket, and a set of dice that shall deceive the devil.

Stu. That fellow has a head to undo a nation. But for the rest, they are such low-mannered, ill-looking dogs, I wonder Beverley has not suspected them.

Bates. No matter for manners and looks: do You supply them with money, and they are gentlemen by profession. The passion of gaming casts such a mist before the eyes, that the nobleman shall be surrounded with sharpers, and imagine himself in the best company.

Stu. There's that Williams too: it was He, I suppose, that called at Beverley's with the note this morning. What directions did you give him?

435Kkk2

Bates. To knock loud, and be clamorous. Did not you see him?

Stu. No. The fool sneaked off with Jarvis. Had he appeared within-doors, as directed, the note had been discharged. I waited there on purpose. I want the women to think well of me; for Lewson's grown suspicious; he told me so himself.

Bates. What answer did you make him?

Stu. A short one. That I would see him soon, for farther explanation.

Bates. We must take care of him. But what have we to do with Beverley? Dawson and the rest are wondering at you.

Stu. Why let them wonder. I have designs above Their narrow reach. They see me lend him money; and they stare at me. But they are fools. I want him to believe me beggared by him.

Bates. And what then?

Stu. Ay, there's the question; but no matter. At night you may know more. He waits for me at Wilson's. I told the women where to find him.

Bates. To what purpose?

Stu. To save suspicion. It looked friendly; and they thanked me. Old Jarvis was dispatched to him.

Bates. And may intreat him home.

Stu. No; he expects money from me: but I'll have none. His wife's jewels must go. Women are easy creatures, and refuse nothing where they love. Follow me to Wilson's; but besure he sees you not. You are a man of character, you know; of prudence and discretion. Wait for me 436 in an outer room; I shall have business for you presently. Come, Sir.

Let drudging fools by honesty grow great;
The shorter road to riches is deceit.

[*Exeunt.*

437

ACT II.

SCENE a gaming house, with a table, box, dice, &c.

Beverley is discovered sitting.

BEVERLEY.

WHY, what a world is this! The slave that digs for gold, receives his daily pittance, and sleeps contented; while those, for whom he labours, convert their good to mischief; making abundance the means of want. O shame! shame! Had fortune given me but a little, that little had been still my own. But plenty leads to waste; and shallow streams maintain their currents, while swelling rivers beat down their banks, and leave their channels empty. What had I to do with play? I wanted nothing. My wishes and my means were equal. The poor followed me with blessings; love scattered roses on my pillow, and morning waked me to delight. — O, bitter thought! that leads to what I was, by what I am! I would forget both — Who's there?

SCENE II.

Enter a Waiter.

Wait. A gentleman, Sir, enquires for you.

Bev. He might have used less ceremony. Stukely I suppose?

Wait. No, Sir; a stranger.

438

Bev. Well, shew him in. (*Exit Waiter.*) A messenger from Stukely then. From Him that has undone me! Yet all in friendship; and now he lends me from his little, to bring back fortune to me.

SCENE III.

Enter Jarvis.

Jarvis! Why this intrusion? — Your absence had been kinder.

Jar. I came in duty, Sir. If it be troublesome —

Bev. It is. I would be private; hid even from myself. Who sent you hither?

Jar. One that would persuade you home again. My mistress is not well; her tears told me so.

Bev. Go with thy duty there then. But does she weep? I am to blame to let her weep. Prithee begone; I have no business for thee.

Jar. Yes, Sir; to lead you from this place. I am your servant still. Your prosperous fortune blessed my old age. If That has left you, I must not leave you.

Bev. Not leave me! Recall past time then; or through this sea of storms and darkness, shew me a star to guide me. But what can'st Thou?

Jar. The little that I can, I will. You have been generous to me. I would not offend you, Sir — but —

Bev. No. Think'st thou I'd ruin Thee too? I have enough of shame already. My wife! my wife! Would'st thou believe it, Jarvis? I have not seen her all this long night; I, who have loved her so, that every hour of abscence seemed as a gap in life. But other bonds have held me. O! I have played the boy; dropping my counters in 439 the stream, and reaching to redeem them, have lost Myself. Why wilt Thou follow misery? Or if thou wilt, go to thy mistress — She has no guilt to sting her, and therefore may be comforted.

Jar. For pity's sake, Sir! I have no heart to see this change.

Bev. Nor I to bear it. How speaks the world of me, Jarvis?

Jar. As of a good man dead. Of one, who walking in a dream, fell down a precipice. The world is sorry for you.

Bev. Ay, and pities me. Says it not so? But I was born to infamy. I'll tell thee what it says. It calls me villain; a treacherous husband; a cruel father; a false brother; one lost to nature and her charities—Or to say all in one short word, it calls me—Gamester. Go to thy mistress; I'll see her presently.

Jar. And why not now? Rude people press upon her; loud, bawling creditors; wretches, who know no pity. I met one at the door; he would have seen my mistress—I wanted means of present payment, so promised it to-morrow. But others may be pressing; and she has grief enough already. Your absence hangs too heavy on her.

Bev. Tell her I'll come then. I have a moment's business. But what hast Thou to do with My distresses? Thy honesty has left thee poor; and age wants comfort. Keep what thou hast for cordials; left between thee and the grave, misery steal in. I have a friend shall counsel me—This is that friend.

440

SCENE IV.

Enter Stukely.

Stu. How fares it, Beverley? Honest Mr. Jarvis, well met; I hoped to find you here. That viper Williams! Was it not He that troubled you this morning?

Jar. My mistress heard him then? I am sorry that she heard him.

Bev. And Jarvis promised payment.

Stu. That must not be. Tell him I'll satisfy him.

Jar. Will you, Sir? Heaven will reward you for't.

Bev. Generous Stukely! Friendship like yours, had it ability like will, would more than ballance the wrongs of fortune.

Stu. You think too kindly of me. Make haste to Williams; his clamours may be rude else.

[*To Jarvis.*

Jar. And my master will go home again. Alas! Sir, we know of hearts there breaking for his absence.

[*Exit.*

Bev. Would I were dead!

Stu. Or turned hermit; counting a string of beads in a dark cave; or under a weeping willow, praying for mercy on the wicked. Ha! ha! ha! Prithee be a man, and leave dying to disease and old age. Fortune may be ours again; at least, we'll try for't.

Bev. No, it has fooled us on too far.

Stu. Ay, ruined us; and therefore we'll sit down contented. These are the despondings of men without money; but let the shining ore chink in the pocket, and folly turns to wisdom. We are fortune's children. True, she's a fickle mother; but shall We droop because She's peevish? No; she has smiles in store. And these her frowns are meant to brighten them.

441Lll

Bev. Is this a time for levity? But You are single in the ruin, and therefore may talk lightly of it. With Me 'tis complicated misery,

Stu. You censure me unjustly. I but assumed these spirits to chear my friend. Heaven knows he wants a comforter.

Bev. What new misfortune?

Stu. I would have brought you money; but lenders want securities. What's to be done? All that was mine is yours already.

Bev. And there's the weight that sinks me. I have undone my friend too; one, who to save a drowning wretch, reached out his hand, and perished with him.

Stu. Have better thoughts.

Bev. Whence are they to proceed? I have nothing left.

Stu. (Sighing) Then we're indeed undone. What, nothing? No move-ables? nor useless trinkets? Bawbles, locked up in caskets, to starve their owners? I have ventured deeply for you.

Bev. Therefore this heart-ake; for I am lost beyond all hope.

Stu. No : means may be found to save us. Jarvis is rich. Who made him so? This is no time for ceremony.

Bev. And is it for dishonesty? The good old man! Shall I rob Him too? My friend would grieve for't. No; let the little that he has, buy food and cloathing for him.

Stu. Good morning then.

[*Going.*

Bev. So hasty! Why, then good morning.

Stu. And when we meet again, upbraid me. Say it was I that tempted you. Tell Lewson so; and tell him I have wronged you: he has suspicions of me, and will thank you.

Bev, No; we have been companions in a rash voyage, 442 and the same storm has wrecked us both. Mine shall be self-upbraidings.

Stu. And will they feed us? You deal unkindly by me. I have sold and borrowed for you, while land or credit lasted; and now, when fortune should be tried, and my heart whispers me success, I am deserted; turned loose to beggary, while You have hoards.

Bev. What hoards? Name them, and take them.

Stu. Jewels.

Bev. And shall this thriftless hand seize Them too? My poor, poor wife! Must she lose all? I would not wound her so.

Stu. Nor I, but from necessity. One effort more, and fortune may grow kind. I have unusual hopes.

Bev. Think of some other means then.

Stu. I have; and you rejected them.

Bev. Prithee let me be a man.

Stu. Ay, and your friend a poor one. But I have done. And for these trinkets of a woman, why, let her keep them to deck out pride with, and shew a laughing world that she has finery to starve in.

Bev. No; she shall yield up all. My friend demands it. But need he have talked lightly of her? The jewels that She values are truth and innocence: those will adorn her ever; and for the rest, she wore them for a husband's pride, and to his wants will give them. Alas! you know her not. Where shall we meet?

Stu. No matter. I have changed my mind. Leave me to a prison; 'tis the reward of friendship.

Bev. Perish mankind first! Leave you to a prison! No: fallen as you see me, I'm not that wretch. Nor would I change this heart, over-charged as 'tis with folly and misfortune, 443Lll2 for one most prudent and most happy, if callous to a friend's distresses.

Stu. You are too warm.

Bev. In such a cause, not to be warm is to be frozen. Farewell. I'll meet you at your lodgings.

Stu. Reflect a little. The jewels may be lost. Better not hazard them. I was too pressing.

Bev. And I ungrateful. Reflection takes up time. I have no leisure for't. Within an hour expect me.

[*Exit.*

Stu. The thoughtless, shallow prodigal! We shall have sport at night then—But hold—the jewels are not ours yet. The lady may refuse them. The husband may relent too. 'Tis more than probable— I'll write a note to Beverley, and the contents shall spur him to demand them. But am I grown this rogue through avarice? No; I have warmer motives: love and revenge. Ruin the husband, and the wife's virtue may be bid for. 'Tis of uncertain value, and sinks, or rises in the purchase, as want, or wealth, or passion governs. The poor part cheaply with it; rich dames, though pleased with selling, will have high prices for't; your love-sick girls give it for oaths and lying; but wives, who boast of honour and affections, keep it against a famine. Why, let the famine come then; I am in haste to purchase.

SCENE V.

Enter Bates.

Look to your men, Bates; there's money stirring. We meet to-night upon this spot. Hasten and tell them so. Beverley calls upon me at my lodgings, and we return together. Hasten, I say; the rogues will scatter else. 444

Bates. Not till their leader bids them.

Stu. Come on then. Give them the word, and follow me; I must advise with you. This is a day of business.

[*Exeunt.*

SCENE VI. changes to Beverley's lodgings.

Enter Beverley, and Charlotte.

Char. Your looks are changed too; there's wildness in them. My wretched sister! how will it grieve her to see you thus!

Bev. No, no; a little rest will ease me. And for your Lewson's kindness to her, it has my thanks: I have no more to give him.

Char. Yes; a sister and her fortune. I trifle with him; and he complains. My looks, he says, are cold upon him. He thinks too—

Bev. That I have *lost* your fortune—He dares not think so.

Char. Nor does he—You are too quick at guessing. He cares not if you had. That care is mine. I lent it you to husband; and now I claim it.

Bev. You have suspicions then?

Char. Cure them, and give it me.

Bev. To stop a sister's chiding.

Char. To vindicate her brother.

Bev. How if he needs it not?

Char. I would fain hope so.

Bev. Ay, would and cannot. Leave it to time then; 'twill satisfy all doubts.

Char. Mine are already satisfied.

Bev. 'Tis well. And when the subject is renewed, speak to me like a sister, and I will answer like a brother.

445Lll3

Char. To tell me I'm a beggar. Why, tell it now. I that can bear the ruin of those dearer to me, the ruin of a sister and her infant, can bear that too.

Bev. No more of this—You wring my heart.

Char. Would that the misery were all your own! But innocence must suffer. Unthinking rioter! whose home was heaven to him: an angel dwelt there, and a little cherub, that crowned his days with blessings—How has he lost this heaven, to league with devils!

Bev. Forbear, I say; reproaches come too late; they search, but cure not. And for the fortune you demand, we'll talk to-morrow on't; our tempers may be milder.

Char. Or if 'tis gone, why, farewel all. I claimed it for a sister. She holds my heart in hers; and every pang She feels, tears it in pieces— But I'll upbraid no more. What heaven permits, it may ordain; and sorrow then is sinful. Yet that the husband! father! brother! should be its instrument of vengeance!—'Tis grievous to know that.

Bev. If you're my sister, spare the remembrance—It wounds too deeply. To-morrow shall clear all; and when the worst is known, it may be better than your fears. Comfort my wife; and for the pains of absence, I'll make atonement. The world may yet go well with us.

Char. See where she comes!—Look chearfully upon her. Affections, such as hers, are prying; and lend those eyes that read the soul.

SCENE VII.

Enter Mrs. Beverley, and Lewson.

Mrs. Bev. My life!

Bev. My love! How fares it? I have been a truant husband.

Mrs. Bev. But we meet now, and that heals all. Doubts and alarms I have had; but in this dear embrace I bury and forget them. My friend here (*pointing to Lewson*) has been indeed a friend. Charlotte, 'tis You must thank him: your brother's thanks and mine are of too little value.

Bev. Yet what we have, we'll pay. I thank, you, Sir, and am obliged. I would say more, but that your goodness to the wife, up-braids the husband's follies. Had I been wise, She had not trespassed on your bounty.

Lew. Nor has she trespassed. The little I have done, acceptance over-pays.

Char. So friendship thinks—

Mrs. Bev. And doubles obligations, by striving to conceal them—We'll talk another time on't. You are too thoughtful, love.

Bev. No; I have reason for these thoughts.

Char. And hatred for the cause. Would you had that too!

Bev. I have. The cause was avarice.

Char. And who the tempter?

Bev. A ruined friend. Ruined by too much kindness,

Lew. Ay, worse than ruined; stabbed in his fame; mortally stabbed. Riches can't cure him.

Bev. Or if they could, those I have drained him of. Something of this he hinted in the morning—that Lewson had suspicions of him—Why these suspicions?

[*Angrily.*

Lew. At school we knew this Stukely. A cunning plodding boy he was, sordid and cruel. Slow at his talk, but quick at shifts and tricking. He schemed out mischief, that others might be punished; and would tell his tale with so much art, that for the lash he merited, rewards 447 and praise were given him. Shew me a boy with such a mind, and time that ripens manhood in him, shall ripen vice too. I'll prove him, and lay him open t'you. Till then be warned. I know him, and therefore shun him.

Bev. As I would those that wrong him. You are too busy, Sir.

Mrs. Bev. No, not too busy—Mistaken perhaps—That had been milder.

Lew. No matter, madam. I can bear this, and praise the heart that prompts it. Pity such friendship should be so placed!

Bev. Again, Sir!—But I'll bear too. You wrong him, Lewson, and will be sorry for't.

Char. Ay, when 'tis proved he wrongs him. The world is full of hypocrites.

Bev. And Stukely one—So you'd infer, I think. I'll hear no more of this—My heart akes for him—I have undone him.

Lew. The world says otherwise.

Bev. The world is false then. I have business with you, love. (*To Mrs. Beverley.*) We'll leave them to their rancour.

[*Going.*

Char. No. We shall find room within for't. Come this way, Sir.

[*To Lewson.*

Lew. Another time my friend will thank me; that time is hastening too.

[*Exit with Charlotte.*

Bev. They hurt me beyond bearing. Is Stukely false? Then honesty has left us!

'Twere sinning against heaven to think so.

Mrs. Bev. I never doubted him.

Bev. No; You are charity. Meekness and ever-during patience live in that heart, and love that knows no change—Why did I ruin you?

448

Mrs. Bev. You have not ruined me. I have no wants when You are present, nor wishes in your absence, but to be blest with your return. Be but resigned to what has happened, and I am rich beyond the dreams of avarice.

Bev. My generous girl! — But memory will be busy; still crowding on my thoughts, to sour the present by the past. I have another pang too.

Mrs. Bev. Tell it, and let me cure it.

Bev. That friend, that generous friend, whose fame they have traduced — I have undone Him too. While he had means, he lent me largely; and now a prison must be his portion.

Mrs. Bev. No; I hope otherwise.

Bev. To hope must be to act. The charitable wish feeds not the hungry. Something must be done.

Mrs. Bev. What?

Bev. In bitterness of heart he told me, just now he told me, I had undone him. Could I hear that, and think of happiness? No; I have disclaimed it, while He is miserable.

Mrs. Bev. The world may mend with us, and then we may be grateful. There's comfort in that hope.

Bev. Ay; 'tis the sick man's cordial, his promised cure; while in preparing it, the patient dies. — What now?

SCENE VIII.

Enter Lucy.

Lucy. A letter, Sir.

[*Delivers it, and exit.*

Bev. The hand is Stukely's.

[*Opens, and reads it to himself.*

Mrs. Bev. And brings good news — at least I'll hope so — What says he, love?

449Mmm

Bev. Why, this—too much for patience. Yet he directs me to conceal it from you.

[*Reads.*

> *Let your haste to see me be the only proof of your esteem*
> *for me. I have determined, since we parted, to bid adieu*
> *to England; chusing rather to forsake my country, than*
> *to owe my freedom in it to the means we talked of. Keep*
> *this a secret at home, and hasten to the ruined*

R. Stukely

Ruined by friendship! I must relieve, or follow him.

Mrs. Bev. Follow him, did you say? Then I am lost indeed!

Bev. O this infernal vice! how has it sunk me! A vice, whose highest joy was poor to my domestic happiness. Yet how have I pursued it! Turned all my comforts to bitterest pangs! and all Thy smiles to tears. Damned, damned infatuation!

Mrs. Bev. Be cool, my life! What are the means the letter talks of? Have You, have I those means? Tell me, and ease me. I have no life while You are wretched.

Bev. No, no; it must not be. 'Tis I alone have sinned; 'tis I alone must suffer. You shall reserve those means, to keep my child and his wronged mother from want and wretchedness.

Mrs. Bev. What means?

Bev. I came to rob you of them; but cannot—dare not; those jewels are your sole support—I should be more than monster to request them.

Mrs. Bev. My jewels! Trifles, not worth the speaking of, if weighed against a husband's peace; but let them purchase That, and the world's wealth is of less value.

450

Bev. Amazing goodness! How little do I seem before such virtues!

Mrs. Bev. No more, my love. I kept them till occasion called to use them; now is the occasion, and I'll resign them chearfully.

Bev. Why, we'll be rich in love then—But this excess of kindness melts me. Yet for a friend one would do much. He has denied Me nothing.

Mrs. Bev. Come to my closet—But let him manage wisely. We have no more to give him.

Bev. Where learnt my love this excellence? 'Tis heaven's own teaching; that heaven, which to an angel's form, has given a mind more lovely. I am unworthy of you, but will deserve you better.

Henceforth my follies and neglects shall cease,
And all to come be penitence and peace;
Vice shall no more attract me with her charms,
Nor pleasure reach me, but in these dear arms.

[*Exeunt.*

451Mmm2

ACT III.

SCENE I. Stukely's lodgings.

Enter Stukely, and Bates.

STUKELY.

SO runs the world, Bates. Fools are the natural prey of knaves; nature designed them so, when she made lambs for wolves. The laws that fear and policy have framed, nature disclaims: she knows but two; and those are force and cunning. The nobler law is force; but then there's danger in't; while cunning, like a skilful miner, works safely and unseen.

Bat. And therefore wisely. Force must have nerves and sinews; cunning wants neither. The dwarf that has it, shall trip the giant's heels up.

Stu. And bind him to the ground. Why, we'll erect a shrine for nature, and be her oracles. Conscience is weakness; fear made, and fear maintains it. The dread of shame, inward reproaches, and fictitious burnings, swell out the phantom. Nature knows none of this; Her laws are freedom.

Bat. Sound doctrine, and well delivered!

Stu. We are sincere too, and practice what we teach. Let the grave pedant say as much—But now to business. The jewels are disposed of; and Beverley again worth money. He waits to count his gold out, and then comes hither. If my design succeeds, this night we finish with 452 him. Go to your lodgings, and be busy. You understand conveyances, and can make ruin sure.

Bat. Better stop here. The sale of this reversion may be talked of; there's danger in't.

Stu. No; 'tis the mark I aim at. We'll thrive, and laugh. You are the purchaser, and there's the payment. (*Giving a pocket book.*) He thinks you rich; and so you shall be. Enquire for titles, and deal hardly; 'twill look like honesty.

Bat. How if he suspects us?

Stu. Leave it to Me. I study hearts, and when to work upon them. Go to your lodgings; and if we come, be busy over papers. Talk of a thoughtless age, of gaming and extravagance, you have a face for't.

Bat. A feeling too that would avoid it. We push too far; but I have cautioned you. If it ends ill, you'll think of me; and so adieu.

[*Exit.*

Stu. This fellow sins by halves; his fears are conscience

to him. I'll turn these fears to use. Rogues that dread shame, will still be greater rogues to hide their guilt—This shall be thought of. Lewson grows troublesome—we must get rid of him—he knows too much. I have a tale for Beverley; part of it truth too. He shall call Lewson to account. If it succeeds, 'tis well; if not, we must try other means—But here he comes—I must dissemble.

SCENE II.

Enter Beverley.

Look to the door there! (*In a seeming fright.*)—My friend!—I thought of other visitors.

Bev. No: these shall guard you from them. (*Offering 453 notes*) Take them, and use them cautiously. The world deals hardly by us.

Stu. And shall I leave you destitute? No: Your wants are greatest. Another climate may treat me kinder. The shelter of to-night takes me from this.

Bev. Let these be your support then. Yet is there need of parting? I may have means again; we'll share them, and live wisely.

Stu. No. I should tempt you on. Habit is nature in me; ruin can't cure it. Even now I would be gaming. Taught by experience as I am, and knowing this poor sum is all that's left us, I am for venturing still. And say I am to blame; yet will this little supply our wants? No; we must put it out to usury. Whether 'tis madness in me, or some resistless impulse of good fortune, I yet am ignorant; but —

Bev. Take it, and succeed then. I'll try no more.

Stu. 'Tis surely impulse; it pleads so strongly — But You are cold — we'll e'en part here then. And for this last reserve, keep it for better uses; I'll have none on't. I thank you though, and will seek fortune singly — One thing I had forgot —

Bev. What is it?

Stu. Perhaps, 'twere best forgotten. But I am open in my nature, and zealous for the honour of my friend — Lewson speaks freely of you.

Bev. Of You I know he does.

Stu. I can forgive him for't; but for my friend I'm angry.

Bev. What says he of me?

Stu. That Charlotte's fortune is embezzled. He talks on't loudly.

454

Bev. He shall be silenced then — How heard you of it?

Stu. From many. He questioned Bates about it. You must account with him, he says.

Bev. Or He with Me — and soon too.

Stu. Speak mildly to him. Cautions are best.

Bev. I'll think on't — But whither go you?

Stu. From poverty and prisons—No matter whither. If fortune changes you may hear from me.

Bev. May these be prosperous then. (*Offering the notes, which he refuses*) Nay, they are yours; I have sworn it, and will have nothing. Take them and use them.

Stu. Singly I will not. My cares are for my friend; for his lost fortune, and ruined family. All separate interests I disclaim. Together we have fallen; together we must rise. My heart, my honour, both will have it so.

Bev. I am weary of being fooled.

Stu. And so am I. Here let us part then. These bodings of good-fortune shall be stifled; I'll call them folly, and forget them. This one embrace, and then farewel.

[*Offering to embrace.*

Bev. No; stay a moment—How my poor heart's distracted! I have these bodings too; but whether caught from You, or prompted by my good or evil genius, I know not—The trial shall determine—And yet, my wife—

Stu. Ay, ay, she'll chide.

Bev. No; My chidings are all here.

[*Pointing to his heart.*

Stu. I'll not persuade you.

Bev. I *am* persuaded; by reason too; the strongest reason—necessity. Oh! could I once regain the height I have fallen from, heaven should forsake me in my latest hour, if I again mixed in these scenes, or sacrificed the husband's peace, his joy and best affections to avarice and infamy!

455

Stu. I have resolved like You; and since our motives are so honest, why should we fear success?

Bev. Come on then. Where shall we meet?

Stu, At Wilson's — Yet if it hurts you, leave me: I have misled you often.

Bev. We have misled each other — But come! Fortune is fickle, and may be tired with plaguing us. There let us rest our hopes.

Stu. Yet think a little.

Bev. I cannot — Thinking but distracts me.

When desperation leads, all thoughts are vain;
Reason would lose, what rashness may obtain.

[*Exeunt.*

SCENE III. Beverley's lodgings.

Enter Mrs. Beverley, and Charlotte.

Char. 'Twas all a scheme, a mean one; unworthy of my brother.

Mrs. Bev. No, I am sure it was not. Stukely is honest too; I know he is. This madness has undone them both.

Char. My brother irrecoverably. You are too spiritless a wife — A mournful tale, mixt with a few kind words, will steal away your soul. The world's too subtle for such goodness. Had I been by, he should have asked your life sooner than those jewels.

Mrs. Bev. He should have had it then. (*Warmly*) I live but to oblige him. She who can love, and is beloved like Me, will do as much. Men have done more for mistresses, and women for a base deluder. And shall a wife do less? Your chidings hurt me, Charlotte.

456

Char. And come too late; they might have saved you else. How could he use you so?

Mrs. Bev. 'Twas friendship did it. His heart was breaking for a friend.

Char. The friend that has betrayed him.

Mrs. Bev. Prithee don't think so.

Char. To-morrow he accounts with Me.

Mrs. Bev. And fairly: I will not doubt it.

Char. Unless a friend has wanted—I have no patience—Sister! sister! we are bound to curse this friend.

Mrs. Bev. My Beverley speaks nobly of him.

Char. And Lewson truly—But I displease you with this talk—To-morrow will instruct us.

Mrs. Bev. Stay till it comes then. I would not think so hardly.

Char. Nor I, but from conviction. Yet we have hope of better days. My uncle is infirm, and of an age that threatens hourly. Or if he lives, You never have offended him; and for distresses so unmerited, he will have pity.

Mrs. Bev. I know it, and am chearful. We have no more to lose; and for what's gone, if it brings prudence home, the purchase is well made,

Char. My Lewson will be kind too. While he and I have life and means, You shall divide with us—And see, he's here.

SCENE IV.

Enter Lewson.

We were just speaking of you.

Lew. 'Tis best to interrupt you then. Few characters will bear a scrutiny; and where the bad out-weighs the good, he's safest that's least talked of. What say you, madam?

[*To Charlotte.*

457Nnn

Char. That I hate scandal, though a woman; therefore talk seldom of you.

Mrs. Bev. Or, with more truth, that, though a woman, she loves to praise; therefore talks always of you. I'll leave you to decide it.

[*Exit.*

Lew. How good and amiable! I came to talk in private with you; of matters that concern you.

Char. What matters?

Lew. First answer me sincerely to what I ask.

Char. I will—But you alarm me.

Lew. I am too grave, perhaps; but be assured of this, I have no news that troubles Me, and therefore should not You.

Char. I am easy then. Propose your question.

Lew. 'Tis now a tedious twelve-month, since with an open and kind heart, you said you loved me.

Char. So tedious, did you say?

Lew. And when in consequence of such sweet words, I pressed for marriage, you gave a voluntary promise, that you would live for Me.

Char. You think me changed then?

[*Angrily.*

Lew. I did not say so. A thousand times I have pressed for the performance of this promise; but private cares, a brother's and a sister's ruin, were reasons for delaying it.

Char. I had no other reasons—Where will this end?

Lew. It shall end presently.

Char. Go on, Sir.

Lew. A promise, such as this, given freely, not extorted, the world thinks binding; but I think otherwise.

Char. And would release me from it?

Lew. You are too impatient, madam.

Char. Cool, Sir—quite cool—Pray go on.

458

Lew. Time, and a near acquaintance with my faults, may have brought change: if it be so; or, for a moment, if you have wished this promise were unmade, here I acquit you of it. This is my question then; and with such plainness as I ask it, I shall entreat an answer. Have you repented of this promise?

Char. Stay, Sir. The man that can *suspect* me, shall *find* me changed. Why am I doubted?

Lew. My doubts are of myself. I have my faults, and You have observation. If from my temper, my words or actions, you have conceived a thought against me, or even a wish for separation, all that has passed is nothing.

Char. You startle me—But tell me—I must be answered first. Is it from honour you speak this? or do you wish me changed?

Lew. Heaven knows I do not. Life and my Charlotte are so connected, that to lose one, were loss of both. Yet for a promise, though given in love, and meant for binding; if time, or accident, or reason should change opinion, with Me that promise has no force.

Char. Why, now I'll answer you. Your doubts are prophecies—I am really changed.

Lew. Indeed!

Char. I could torment You now, as You have Me; but 'tis not in my nature. That I am changed I own; for what at first was inclination, is now grown reason in me; and from that reason, had I the world—nay, were I poorer than the poorest, and You too wanting bread; with but a hovel to invite me to—I would be yours, and happy.

Lew. My kindest Charlotte! (*Seizing her hand*) Thanks are too poor for this, and words too weak! But if we love so, why should our union be delayed?

459Nnn2

Char. For happier times. The present are too wretched.

Lew. I may have reasons, that press it now.

Char. What reasons?

Lew. The strongest reasons; unanswerable ones.

Char. Be quick and name them.

Lew. No, madam; I am bound in honour to make conditions first; I am bound by inclination too. This sweet profusion of kind words pains while it pleases. I dread the losing you.

Char. Astonishment! What mean you?

Lew. First promise, that to-morrow, or the next day, you will be mine for ever.

Char. I do—though misery should succeed.

Lew. Thus then I seize you! and with you every joy on this side heaven!

[*Embracing her.*

Char. And thus I seal my promise. (*Returning his embrace.*) Now, Sir, your secret?

Lew. Your fortune's lost.

Char. My fortune lost!—I'll study to be humble then. But was my promise claimed for this? How nobly generous! Where learnt you this sad news?

Lew. From Bates, Stukely's prime agent. I have obliged him, and he's grateful. He told it me in friendship, to warn me from my Charlotte.

Char. 'Twas honest in him; and I'll esteem him for't.

Lew. He knows much more than he has told.

Char. For Me it is enough. And for your generous love, I thank you from my soul. If you'd oblige me more, give me a little time.

Lew. Why time? It robs us of our happiness.

Char. I have a task to learn first. The little pride this fortune gave me, must be subdued. Once we were equal; 460 and might have met obliging and obliged. But now 'tis otherwise; and for a life of obligations, I have not learnt to bear it.

Lew. Mine is that life. You are too noble.

Char. Leave me to think on't.

Lew. To-morrow then you'll fix my happiness?

Char. All that I can, I will.

Lew. It must be so; we live but for each other. Keep what you know a secret; and when we meet to-morrow, more may be known. Farewell.

[*Exit.*

Char. My poor, poor sister! how would this wound her! But I'll conceal it, and speak comfort to her.

[*Exit.*

SCENE V. changes to a room in the gaming-house.

Enter Beverley, and Stukely.

Bev. Whither would you lead me?

[*Angrily.*

Stu. Where we may vent our curses.

Bev. Ay, on yourself, and those damned counsels that have destroyed me. A thousand fiends were in that bosom, and all let loose to tempt me—I had resisted else.

Stu. Go on, Sir. I have deserved this from you.

Bev. And curses everlasting. Time is too scanty for them.

Stu. What have I done?

Bev. What the arch-devil of old did—soothed with false hopes, for certain ruin.

Stu. Myself unhurt; nay, pleased at your destruction—So your words mean. Why, tell it to the world: I am too poor to find a friend in't.

461

Bev. A friend! What's he? I had a friend.

Stu. And have one still.

Bev. Ay; I'll tell you of this friend. He found me happiest of the happy; fortune and honour crowned me; and love and peace lived in my heart. One spark of folly lurked there; That too he found; and by deceitful breath, blew it to flames that have consumed me. This friend were You to Me.

Stu. A little more perhaps—The friend who gave his all to save you; and not succeeding, chose ruin with you. But no matter—I have undone you, and am a villain.

Bev. No; I think not. The villains are within.

Stu. What villains?

Bev. Dawson and the rest—We have been dupes to sharpers.

Stu. How know you this? I have had doubts, as well as You; yet still as fortune changed, I blushed at my own thoughts. But You have proofs, perhaps?

Bev. Ay, damned ones. Repeated losses: night after night, and no reverse. Chance has no hand in this.

Stu. I think more charitably; yet I am peevish in my nature, and apt to doubt. The world speaks fairly of this Dawson; so does it of the rest. We have watched them closely too. But 'tis a right usurped by losers, to think the winners knaves. We'll have more manhood in us.

Bev. I know not what to think. This night has stung me to the quick—blasted my reputation too. I have bound my honour to these vipers; played meanly upon credit, till I tired them; and now they shun me, to rifle one another. What's to be done?

Stu. Nothing. My counsels have been fatal.

Bev. By heaven! I'll not survive this shame—Traitor! 'tis 462 You have brought it on me. (*Taking hold of him.*) Shew me the means to save me, or I'll commit a murder here, and next upon myself.

Stu. Why, do it then, and rid me of ingratitude.

Bev. Prithee, forgive this language—I speak I know not what. Rage and despair are in my heart, and hurry me to madness. My home is horror to me—I'll not return to't. Speak quickly; tell me, if in this wreck of fortune, one hope remains? Name it, and be my oracle.

Stu. To vent your curses on—You have bestowed them liberally. Take your own counsel: and should a desperate hope present itself, 'twill suit your desperate fortune. I'll not advise you.

Bev. What hope? By heaven! I'll catch at it, however desperate. I am so sunk in misery, it cannot lay me lower.

Stu. You have an uncle.

Bev. Ay. What of Him?

Stu. Old men live long by temperance; while their heirs starve on expectation.

Bev. What mean you?

Stu. That the reversion's yours; and will bring money to pay debts with—nay, more; it may retrieve what's past.

Bev. Or leave my child a beggar.

Stu. And what's his father? A dishonourable one; engaged for sums, he cannot pay. That should be thought of.

Bev. It is my shame; the poison that inflames me. Where shall we go? To whom? I am impatient till all's lost.

Stu. All may be yours again. Your man is Bates. He has large funds at his command, and will deal justly by you.

463

Bev. I am resolved—Tell them, within, we'll meet them presently; and with full purses too—Come, follow me.

Stu. No. I'll have no hand in this; nor do I counsel it. Use your discretion, and act from that. You'll find me at my lodgings.

Bev. Succeed what will, this night I'll dare the worst—
  'Tis loss of fear, to be compleatly curs'd.

[*Exit.*

Stu. Why, lose it then for ever. Fear is the mind's worst evil; and 'tis a friendly office to drive it from the bosom. Thus far has fortune crowned me—Yet Beverley is rich; rich in his wife's best treasure; her honour and affections. I would supplant him there too. But 'tis the curse of thinking minds, to raise up difficulties. Fools only conquer women: fearless of dangers which they see not, they press on boldly, and by persisting, prosper. Yet may a tale of art do much. Charlotte is sometimes absent. The seeds of jealousy are sown already: If I mistake not, they have taken root too. Now is the time to ripen them, and reap the harvest. The softest of her sex, if wronged in love, or thinking that she's wronged, becomes a tygress in revenge. I'll instantly to Beverley's—No matter for the danger—When beauty leads us on, 'tis indiscretion to reflect, and cowardice to doubt.

[*Exit.*

SCENE VI. changes to Beverley's lodgings.

Enter Mrs. Beverley, and Lucy.

Mrs. Bev. Did Charlotte tell you any thing?

Lucy. No, madam.

Mrs. Bev. She looked confused methought; said she had business with her Lewson; which, when I pressed to know, tears only were her answer.

464

Lucy. She seemed in haste too: yet her return may bring you comfort.

Mrs. Bev. No, my kind girl; I was not born for't. But why do I distress thee? Thy sympathizing heart bleeds for the ills of others. What pity that thy mistress can't reward thee! But there's a power above, that sees, and will remember all. Prithee, sooth me with the song thou sung'st last night: it suits this change of fortune; and there's a melancholy in't that pleases me.

Lucy. I fear it hurts you, madam. Your goodness too draws tears from me: but I'll dry them, and obey you.

SONG.

When Damon languish'd at my feet,
And I believ'd him true,

The moments of delight how sweet!
But ah! how swift they flew!

The sunny hill, the flow'ry vale,
The garden and the grove,

Have echoed to his ardent tale,
And vows of endless love.

II.

The conquest gain'd, he left his prize,
He left her to complain;

To talk of joy with weeping eyes,
And measure time by pain.

But heav'n will take the mourner's part,
In pity to despair;

And the last sigh that rends the heart,
Shall waft the spirit there.

465Ooo

Mrs. Bev. I thank thee, Lucy; I thank heaven too my griefs are none of these. Yet Stukely deals in hints — He talks of rumours — I'll urge him to speak plainly — Hark? — There's some one entering.

Lucy. Perhaps my master, madam.

[*Exit.*

Mrs. Bev. Let him be well too, and I am satisfied. (*Goes to the door, and listens.*) No; 'tis another's voice; his had been music to me. Who is it, Lucy?

SCENE VII.

Re-enter Lucy with Stukely.

Lucy. Mr. Stukely, madam.

[*Exit.*

Stu. To meet you thus alone, madam, was what I wished. Unseasonable visits, when friendship warrants them, need no excuse; therefore I make none.

Mrs. Bev. What mean you, Sir? And where's your friend?

Stu. Men may have secrets, madam, which their best friends are not admitted to. We parted in the morning, not soon to meet again.

Mrs. Bev. You mean to leave us then? To leave your country too? I am no stranger to your reasons, and pity your misfortunes.

Stu. Your pity has undone you. Could Beverley do this? That letter was a false one; a mean contrivance, to rob you of your jewels. I wrote it not.

Mrs. Bev. Impossible! Whence came it then?

Stu. Wronged as I am, madam, I must speak plainly —

Mrs. Bev. Do so, and ease me. Your hints have troubled me. Reports, you say, are stirring — Reports of whom? You wished me not to credit them. What, Sir, are these reports?

466

Stu. I thought them slander, madam; and cautioned you in friendship; left from officious tongues the tale had reached you, with double aggravation.

Mrs. Bev. Proceed, Sir.

Stu. It is a debt due to my fame, due to an injured wife too — We both are injured.

Mrs. Bev. How injured? and who has injured us?

Stu. My friend, your husband.

Mrs. Bev. You would resent for both then? But know, Sir, My injuries are my own, and do not need a champion.

Stu. Be not too hasty, madam. I come not in resentment, but for acquittance. You thought me poor; and to the feigned distresses of a friend gave up your jewels.

Mrs. Bev. I gave them to a husband.

Stu. Who gave them to a —

Mrs. Bev. What? Whom did he give them to?

Stu. A mistress.

Mrs. Bev. No; on my life he did not.

Stu. Himself confessed it, with curses on her avarice.

Mrs. Bev. I'll not believe it. He has no mistress — or if he has, why is it told to Me?

Stu. To guard you against insults. He told me, that to move you to compliance, he forged that letter, pretending I was ruined; ruined by Him too. The fraud succeeded; and what a trusting wife bestowed in pity, was lavished on a wanton.

Mrs. Bev. Then I am lost indeed; and my afflictions are too powerful for me. His follies I have borne without upbraiding, and saw the approach of poverty without a tear. My affections, my strong affections supported me through every trial.

Stu. Be patient, madam.

467Ooo2

Mrs. Bev. Patient! The barbarous man! And does he think my tenderness of heart is his security for wounding it? But he shall find that injuries such as these, can arm my weakness for vengeance and redress.

Stu. Ha! then I may succeed. (*Aside.*) Redress is in your power.

Mrs. Bev. What redress?

Stu. Forgive me, madam, if in my zeal to serve you, I hazard your displeasure. Think of your wretched state. Already want surrounds you. Is it in patience to bear That? To see your helpless little one robbed of his birth-right? A sister too, with unavailing tears, lamenting her lost fortune? No comfort left you, but ineffectual pity from the Few, out-weighed by insults from the Many?

Mrs. Bev. Am I so lost a creature? Well, Sir, my redress?

Stu. To be resolved is to secure it. The marriage vow, once violated, is in the sight of heaven dissolved — Start not, but hear me! 'Tis now the summer of your youth; time has not cropt the roses from your cheek, though sorrow long has washed them. Then use your beauty wisely; and, freed by injuries, fly from the cruellest of men, for shelter with the kindest.

Mrs. Bev. And who is He?

Stu. A friend to the unfortunate; a bold one too; who while the storm is bursting on your brow, and lightening flashing from your eyes, dares tell you that he loves you.

Mrs. Bev. Would that these eyes had heaven's own lightening! that with a look, thus I might blast thee! Am I then fallen so low? Has poverty so humbled me, that I should listen to a hellish offer, and sell my soul for bread? 468 O, villain! villain! — But now I know thee, and thank thee for the knowledge.

Stu. If you are wife, you shall have cause to thank me.

Mrs. Bev. An injured husband too shall thank thee.

Stu. Yet know, proud woman, I have a heart as stubborn as your own; as haughty and imperious: and as it loves, so can it hate.

Mrs. Bev. Mean, despicable villain! I scorn thee, and thy threats. Was it for this that Beverley was false? That his too credulous wife should in despair and vengeance give up her honour to a wretch? But he shall know it, and vengeance shall be his.

Stu. Why send him for defiance then. Tell him I love his wife; but that a worthless husband forbids our union. I'll make a widow of you, and court you honourably.

Mrs. Bev. O, coward! coward! thy soul will shrink at him. Yet in the thought of what may happen, I feel a woman's fears. Keep thy own secret, and begone. Who's there?

SCENE VIII.

Enter Lucy.

Your absence, Sir, would please me.

Stu. I'll not offend you, madam.

[*Exit with Lucy.*

Mrs. Bev. Why opens not the earth to swallow such a monster? Be conscience then his punisher, till heaven in mercy gives him penitence, or dooms him in its justice.

469

SCENE IX.

Re-enter Lucy.

Come to my chamber, Lucy; I have a tale to tell thee, shall make thee weep for thy poor mistress.

Yet heav'n the guiltless sufferer regards,
And whom it most afflicts, it most rewards.

[*Exeunt.*

470

ACT IV.

SCENE, Beverley's lodgings.

Enter Mrs. Beverley, Charlotte, and Lewson.

CHARLOTTE.

THE smooth-tongued hypocrite!

Lew. But we have found him, and will requite him. Be chearful, madam; (*To Mrs. Beverley*) and for the insults of this ruffian, you shall have ample retribution.

Mrs. Bev. But not by violence—Remember you have sworn it: I had been silent else.

Lew. You need not doubt me; I shall be cool as patience.

Mrs. Bev. See him to-morrow then.

Lew. And why not now? By heaven, the veriest worm that crawls is made of braver spirit than this Stukely. Yet for my promise, I'll deal gently with him. I mean to watch his looks: from those, and from his answers to my charge, much may be learnt. Next I'll to Bates, and sift him to the bottom. If I fail there, the gang is numerous, and for a bribe will each betray the other. Good night; I'll lose no time.

[*Exit.*

Mrs. Bev. These boisterous spirits! how they wound me! But reasoning is in vain. Come, Charlotte; we'll to our usual watch. The night grows late.

471

Char. I am fearful of events; yet pleased—To-morrow may relieve us.

[*Going.*

SCENE II.

Enter Jarvis.

Char. How now, good Jarvis?

Jar. I have heard ill news, madam.

Mrs. Bev. What news? Speak quickly.

Jar. Men are not what they seem. I fear me, Mr. Stukely is dishonest.

Char. We know it, Jarvis. But what's your news?

Jar. That there's an action against my master, at his friend's suit.

Mrs. Bev. O, villain! villain! 'twas this he threatened then. Run to that den of robbers, Wilson's—Your master may be there. Entreat him home, good Jarvis. Say I have business with him—But tell him not of Stukely—It may provoke him to revenge—Haste! haste! good Jarvis.

[*Exit Jarvis.*

Char. This minister of hell! O, I could tear him piece-meal!

Mrs. Bev. I am sick of such a world. Yet heaven is just; and in its own good time, will hurl destruction on such monsters.

[*Exeunt.*

SCENE III. changes to Stukely's lodgings.

Enter Stukely, and Bates, meeting.

Bates. Where have you been?

Stu. Fooling my time away: playing my tricks, like a tame monkey, to entertain a woman—No matter where— 472 I have been vext and disappointed. Tell me of Beverley. How bore he his last shock?

Bates. Like one (so Dawson says) whose senses had been numbed by misery. When all was lost, he fixed his eyes upon the ground, and stood some time, with folded arms, stupid and motionless. Then snatching his sword, that hung against the wainscot, he sat him down; and with a look of fixt attention, drew figures on the floor. At last he started up, looked wild, and trembled; and like a woman, seized with her sex's fits, laughed out aloud, while the tears trickled down his face—so left the room.

Stu. Why, this was madness.

Bates. The madness of despair.

Stu. We must confine him then. A prison would do well. (*A knocking at the door.*) Hark! that knocking may be his. Go that way down. (*Exit Bates.*) Who's there?

SCENE IV.

Enter Lewson.

Lew. An enemy. An open and avowed one.

Stu. Why am I thus broke in upon? This house is mine, Sir; and should protect me from insult and ill-manners.

Lew. Guilt has no place of sanctuary; wherever found, 'tis virtue's lawful game. The fox's hold, and tyger's den, are no security against the hunter.

Stu. Your business, Sir?

Lew. To tell you that I know you—Why this confusion? That look of guilt and terror? Is Beverley awake? Or has his wife told tales? The man that dares like You, 473Ppp should have a soul to justify his deeds, and courage to confront accusers. Not with a coward's fear to shrink beneath reproof.

Stu. Who waits there?

[*Aloud, and in confusion.*

Lew. By heaven, he dies that interrupts us. (*Shutting the door.*) You should have weighed your strength, Sir; and then, instead of climbing to high fortune, the world had marked you for what you are, a little paultry villain.

Stu. You think I fear you.

Lew. I know you fear me. This is to prove it. (*Pulls him by the sleeve.*) You wanted privacy! A lady's presence took up your attention! Now we are alone, Sir. — Why, what a wretch! (*Flings him from him.*) The vilest insect in creation will turn when trampled on; yet has this Thing undone a man — by cunning and mean arts undone him. But we have found you, Sir; traced you through all your labyrinths. If you would save yourself, fall to confession: no mercy will be shewn else.

Stu. First prove me what you think me. Till then, your threatenings are in vain. And for this insult, vengeance may yet be mine.

Lew. Infamous coward! Why, take it now then— (*Draws, and Stukely retires.*) Alas! I pity thee. Yet that a wretch like this should overcome a Beverley! it fills me with astonishment! A wretch, so mean of soul, that even desperation cannot animate him to look upon an enemy. You should not thus have soared, Sir, unless, like others of your black profession, you had a sword to keep the fools in awe, your villainy has ruined.

Stu. Villainy! 'Twere best to curb this licence of your tongue; for know, Sir, while there are laws, this outrage on my reputation will not be borne with.

474

Lew. Laws! Dar'st Thou seek shelter from the laws? those laws, which thou and thy infernal crew live in the constant violation of? Talk'st thou of reputation too? when under friendship's sacred name, thou hast betrayed, robbed, and destroyed?

Stu. Ay, rail at gaming; 'tis a rich topic, and affords noble declamation. Go, preach against it in the city: you'll find a congregation in every tavern. If they should laugh at you, fly to my lord, and sermonize it there: he'll thank you and reform.

Lew. And will example sanctify a vice? No, wretch; the custom of my lord, or of the Cit that apes him, cannot excuse a breach of law, or make the gamester's calling reputable.

Stu. Rail on, I say. But is this zeal for beggared Beverley? Is it for Him that I am treated thus? No; He and His might all have groaned in prison, had but the sister's fortune escaped the wreck, to have rewarded the disinterested love of honest Mr. Lewson.

Lew. How I detest thee for the thought! But thou art lost to every human feeling. Yet let me tell thee, and may it wring thy heart! that though my friend is ruined by thy snares, thou hast unknowingly been kind to Me.

Stu. Have I? It was indeed unknowingly.

Lew. Thou hast assisted me in love; given me the merit that I wanted; since but for Thee, my Charlotte had not known 'twas her dear self I sighed for, and not her fortune.

Stu. Thank me, and take her then.

Lew. And as a brother to poor Beverley, I will pursue the robber that has seized him, and snatch him from his gripe.

Stu. Then know, imprudent man, he *is* within my gripe; 475Ppp2 and should my friendship for him be slandered once again, the hand that has supplied him, shall fall and crush him.

Lew. Why, now there's spirit in thee! This is indeed to be a villain! But I shall reach thee yet. Fly where thou wilt, my vengeance shall pursue thee—and Beverley shall yet be saved, be saved from thee, thou monster; nor owe his rescue to his wife's dishonour.

[*Exit.*

Stu. (*Pausing*) Then ruin has enclosed me. Curse on my coward heart! I would be bravely villainous; but 'tis my nature to shrink at danger, and he has found me. Yet fear brings caution, and That security. More mischief must be done, to hide the past. Look to yourself, officious Lewson—there may be danger stirring—How now, Bates?

SCENE V.

Enter Bates.

Bates. What is the matter? 'Twas Lewson, and not Beverley, that left you. I heard him loud: you seem alarmed too.

Stu. Ay, and with reason. We are discovered.

Bates. I feared as much, and therefore cautioned you; but You were peremptory.

Stu. Thus fools talk ever; spending their idle breath on what is past; and trembling at the future. We must be active. Beverley, at worst, is but suspicious; but Lewson's genius, and his hate to Me, will lay all open. Means must be found to stop him.

Bates. What means?

Stu. Dispatch him—Nay, start not—Desperate occasions call for desperate deeds. We live but by his death.

Bates. You cannot mean it?

476

Stu. I do, by heaven.

Bates. Good night then.

[*Going.*

Stu. Stay. I must be heard, then answered. Perhaps the motion was too sudden; and human nature starts at murder, though strong necessity compels it. I have thought long of this; and my first feelings were like yours; a foolish conscience awed me, which soon I conquered. The man that would undo me, nature cries out, undo. Brutes know their foes by instinct; and where superior force is given, they use it for destruction. Shall man do less? Lewson pursues us to our ruin; and shall we, with the means to crush him, fly from our hunter, or turn and tear him? 'Tis folly even to hesitate.

Bates. He has obliged me, and I dare not.

Stu. Why, live to shame then, to beggary and punishment. You would be privy to the deed, yet want the soul to act it. Nay more; had my designs been levelled at his fortune, you had stept in the foremost. And what is life without its comforts? Those you would rob him of; and by a lingering death, add cruelty to murder. Henceforth adieu to half-made villains—there's danger in them. What you have got is your's; keep it, and hide with it: I'll deal my future bounty to those who merit it.

Bates. What's the reward?

Stu. Equal division of our gains. I swear it, and will be just.

Bates. Think of the means then.

Stu. He's gone to Beverley's — Wait for him in the street — 'tis a dark night, and fit for mischief. A dagger would be useful.

Bates. He sleeps no more.

Stu. Consider the reward! When the deed's done, I have farther business with you. Send Dawson to me.

477

Bates. Think it already done — and so farewel.

[*Exit.*

Stu. Why, farewel Lewson then; and farewel to my fears. This night secures me. I'll wait the event within.

[*Exit.*

SCENE VI. changes to the street. Stage darkened.

Enter Beverley.

Bev. How like an out-cast do I wander! Loaded with every curse, that drives the soul to desperation! The midnight robber, as he walks his rounds, sees by the glimmering lamp my frantic looks, and dreads to meet me. Whither am I going? My home lies there; all that is dear on earth it holds too; yet are the gates of death more welcome to me. I'll enter it no more — Who passes there? Tis Lewson. He meets me in a gloomy hour; and memory tells me, he has been meddling with my fame.

SCENE VII.

Enter Lewson.

Lew. Beverley! Well met. I have been busy in your affairs.

Bev. So I have heard, Sir; and now must thank you for't.

Lew. To-morrow I may deserve your thanks. Late as it is, I go to Bates. Discoveries are making that an arch villain trembles at.

Bev. Discoveries are made, Sir, that You shall tremble at. Where is this boasted spirit? this high demeanour, that was to call me to account? You say I have wronged 478 my sister—Now say as much. But first be ready for defence, as I am for resentment.

[*Draws.*

Lew. What mean you? I understand you not.

Bev. The coward's stale acquittance. Who, when he spreads foul calumny abroad, and dreads just vengeance on him, cries out, what mean you, I understand you not.

Lew. Coward, and calumny! Whence are these words? But I forgive, and pity you.

Bev. Your pity had been kinder to my fame. But you have traduced it; told a vile story to the public ear, that I have wronged my sister.

Lew. 'Tis false. Shew me the man that dares accuse me.

Bev. I thought you brave, and of a soul superior to low malice; but I have found you, and will have vengeance. This is no place for argument.

Lew. Nor shall it be for violence. Imprudent man! who in revenge for fancied injuries, would pierce the heart that loves him! But honest friendship acts from itself, unmoved by slander, or ingratitude. The life you thirst for, shall be employed to serve you.

Bev. 'Tis thus you would compound then! First do a wrong beyond forgiveness; and to redress it, load me with kindness unsolicited. I'll not receive it. Your zeal is troublesbme.

Lew. No matter. It shall be useful.

Bev. It will not be accepted.

Lew. It must. You know me not.

Bev. Yes; for the slanderer of my fame: who under shew of friendship, arraigns me of injustice; buzzing in every ear foul breach of trust, and family dishonour.

Lew. Have I done this? Who told you so?

479

Bev. The world. 'Tis talked of everywhere. It pleased you to add threats too: you were to call me to account — Why, do it now then; I shall be proud of such an arbiter.

Lew. Put up your sword, and know me better. I never injured you. The base suggestion comes from Stukely: I see him and his aims.

Bev. What aims? I'll not conceal it; '*twas* Stukely that accused you.

Lew. To rid him of an enemy: perhaps of two. He fears discovery, and frames a tale of falsehood, to ground revenge and murder on.

Bev. I must have proof of this.

Lew. Wait till to-morrow then.

Bev. I will.

Lew. Good night. I go to serve you. Forget what's past, as I do; and chear your family with smiles. To-morrow may confirm them, and make all happy.

[*Exit.*

Bev. (*Pausing*) How vile, and how absurd is man! His boasted honour is but another name for pride; which easier bears the consciousness of guilt, than the world's just reproofs. But 'tis the fashion of the times; and in defence of falsehood and false honour, men die martyrs. I knew not that my nature was so bad.

[*Stands musing.*

SCENE VIII.

Enter Bates, and Jarvis.

Jar. This way the noise was — and yonder's my poor master.

Bates. I heard him at high words with Lewson. The cause I know not.

480

Jar. I heard him too. Misfortunes vex him.

Bates. Go to him, and lead him home — But he comes this way — I'll not be seen by him.

[*Exit.*

Bev. (*Starting.*) What fellow's that? (*Seeing Jarvis*). Art thou a murderer, friend? Come, lead the way; I have a hand as mischievous as thine; a heart as desperate too — Jarvis! — To bed, old man, the cold will chill thee.

Jar. Why are you wandering at this late hour? — Your sword drawn too! — For heav'n's sake sheath it, Sir; the sight distracts Me.

Bev. Whose voice was that?

[*Wildly.*

Jar. 'Twas mine, Sir. Let me intreat you to give the sword to me.

Bev. Ay, take it; quickly take it — Perhaps I am not so curst, but heav'n may have sent thee at this moment to snatch me from perdition.

Jar. Then I am blest.

Bev. Continue so, and leave me. My sorrows are contagious. No one is blest that's near me.

Jar. I came to seek you, Sir.

Bev. And now thou hast found me, leave me. My thoughts are wild, and will not be disturbed.

Jar. Such thoughts are best disturbed.

Bev. I tell thee that they will not. Who sent thee hither?

Jar. My weeping mistress.

Bev. Am I so meek a husband then? that a commanding wife prescribes my hours, and sends to chide me for my absence? Tell her, I'll not return.

Jar. Those words would kill her.

Bev. Kill her! Would they not be kind then? But she shall live to curse me — I have deserved it of her. Does she not hate me, Jarvis?

481Qqq

Jar. Alas, Sir! Forget your griefs, and let me lead you to her. The streets are dangerous.

Bev. Be wise, and leave me then. The night's black horrors are suited to my thoughts. These stones shall be my resting-place. (*Lies down.*) Here shall my soul brood o'er its miseries; till with the fiends of hell, and guilty of the earth, I start and tremble at the morning's light.

Jar. For pity's sake, Sir!—Upon my knees I beg you to quit this place, and these sad thoughts. Let patience, not despair, possess you. Rise, I beseech you. There's not a moment of your absence, that my poor mistress does not groan for.

Bev. Have I undone her, and is she still so kind? (*Starting up*) It is too much—My brain can't hold it—O, Jarvis! Jarvis! how desperate is that wretch's state, which only death or madness can relieve!

Jar. Appease his mind, good heaven! and give him resignation! Alas, Sir, could beings in the other world perceive the events of this, how would your parents' blessed spirits grieve for you, even in heaven! Let me conjure you by Their honoured memories; by the sweet innocence of your yet helpless child, and by the ceaseless sorrows of my poor mistress, to rouze your manhood, and struggle with these griefs.

Bev. Thou virtuous, good old man! thy tears and thy entreaties have reached my heart, through all its miseries. O! had I listened to Thy honest warnings, no earthly blessing had been wanting to me! I was so happy, that even a wish for more than I possessed, was arrogant presumption. But I have warred against the power that blest me, and now am sentenced to the hell I merit.

Jar. Be but resigned, Sir, and happiness may yet be yours.

482

Bev. Prithee be honest, and do not flatter misery.

Jar. I do not, Sir—Hark! I hear voices—Come this way; we may reach home un-noticed.

Bev. Well, lead me then—Un-noticed did'st thou say? Alas! I dread no looks, but of those wretches I have made at home.

[*Exeunt.*

SCENE IX. changes to Stukely's.

Enter Stukely, and Dawson.

Stu. Come hither, Dawson. My limbs are on the rack, and my soul shivers in me, till this night's business be complete. Tell me thy thoughts: is Bates determined? or does he waver?

Daw. At first he seemed irresolute; wished the employment had been mine; and muttered curses on his coward hand, that trembled at the deed.

Stu. And did he leave you so?

Daw. No. We walked together; and sheltered by the darkness, saw Beverley and Lewson in warm debate. But soon they cooled; and then I left them, to hasten hither; but not till 'twas resolved Lewson should die.

Stu. Thy words have given me life. That quarrel too was fortunate; for if my hopes deceive me not, it promises a grave to Beverley.

Daw. You misconceive me. Lewson and he were friends.

Stu. But My prolific brain shall make them enemies. If Lewson falls, he falls by Beverley: an upright jury shall decree it. Ask me no questions, but do as I direct. This writ (*Takes out a pocket book*) for some days past, I have treasured here, till a convenient time called for its use. That time is come. Take it, and give it to an officer. It must be served this instant.

[*Gives a paper.*

483Qqq2

Daw. On Beverley?

Stu. Look at it. 'Tis for the sums that I have lent him.

Daw. Must he to prison then?

Stu. I asked obedience; not replies. This night a jail must be his lodging. 'Tis probable he's not gone home yet. Wait at his door, and see it executed.

Daw. Upon a beggar? He has no means of payment.

Stu. Dull and insensible! If Lewson dies, who was it killed him? Why, he that was seen quarrelling with him; and I that knew of Beverley's intents, arrested him in friendship — A little late, perhaps; but 'twas a virtuous act, and men will thank me for it. Now, Sir, you understand me?

Daw. Most perfectly; and will about it.

Stu. Haste then; and when 'tis done, come back and tell me.

Daw. 'Till then farewel.

[*Exit.*

Stu. Now tell thy tale, fond wife! And, Lewson, if again thou can'st insult me, I'll kneel and own thee for my master.

Not av'rice now, but vengeance fires my breast
And one short hour must make me curst, or blest.

[*Exit.*

484

ACT V.

SCENE I. Enter Stukely, Bates, and Dawson.

BATES.

POOR Lewson! But I told you enough last night. The thoughts of him are horrible to me.

Stu. In the street, did you say? And no one near him?

Bates. By his own door; he was leading me to his house. I pretended business with him, and stabbed him to the heart, while he was reaching at the bell.

Stu. And did he fall so suddenly?

Bates. The repetition pleases you, I see. I told you, he fell without a groan.

Stu. What heard you of him this morning?

Bates. That the watch found him in their rounds, and alarmed the servants. I mingled with the crowd just now, and saw him dead in his own house. The sight terrified me.

Stu. Away with terrors, till his ghost rise and accuse us. We have no living enemy to fear—unless 'tis Beverley; and him we have lodged safe in prison.

Bates. Must He be murdered too?

Stu. No; I have a scheme to make the law his murderer. At what hour did Lewson fall?

Bates. The clock struck twelve, just as I turned to leave him. 'Twas a melancholy bell, I thought, tolling for his death.

Stu. The time was lucky for us. Beverley was arrested at one, you say?

[*To Dawson.*

485

Daw. Exactly.

Stu. Good. We'll talk of this presently. The women were with him, I think?

Daw. And old Jarvis. I would have told you of them last night, but your thoughts were too busy. 'Tis well you have a heart of stone, the tale would melt it else.

Stu. Out with it then.

Daw. I traced him to his lodgings; and pretending pity for his misfortunes, kept the door open, while the officers seized him. 'Twas a damned deed—but no matter—I followed my instructions.

Stu. And what said he?

Daw. He upbraided me with treachery, called You a villain, acknowledged the sums you had lent him, and submitted to his fortune.

Stu. And the women—

Daw. For a few minutes astonishment kept them silent. They looked wildly at one another, while the tears streamed down their cheeks. But rage and fury soon gave them words; and then, in the very bitterness of despair, they cursed me, and the monster that had employed me.

Stu. And you bore it with philosophy?

Daw. Till the scene changed, and then I melted. I ordered the officers to take away their prisoner. The women shrieked, and would have followed him; but We forbad them. 'Twas then they fell upon their knees, the wife fainting, the sister raving, and both, with all the eloquence of misery, endeavouring to soften us. I never felt compassion till that moment; and had the officers been moved like Me, we had left the business undone, and fled with curses on ourselves. But their hearts were steeled by 486 custom: the tears of beauty, and the pangs of affection, were beneath their pity. They tore him from their arms, and lodged him in prison, with only Jarvis to comfort him.

Stu. There let him lie, till we have farther business with him. And for You, Sir, let me hear no more of your compassion. A fellow nursed in villainy, and employed from childhood in the business of hell, should have no dealings with compassion.

Daw. Say you so, Sir? You should have named the devil that tempted me.

Stu. 'Tis false. I found you a villain; therefore employed you — But no more of this — We have embarked too far in mischief to recede. Lewson is dead; and we are all principals in his murder. Think of that. There's time enough for pity, when ourselves are out of danger. Beverley still lives, though in a jail. His ruin will sit heavy on him; and discoveries may be made to undo us all. Something must be done, and speedily. You saw him quarrelling with Lewson in the street last night?

[*To Bates.*

Bates. I did; his steward, Jarvis, saw him too.

Stu. And shall attest it. Here's matter to work upon. An unwilling evidence carries weight with him. Something of my design I have hinted t'you before. Beverley must be the author of this murder; and

We the parties to convict him. But how to proceed, will require time and thought—Come along with Me; the room within is fitter for privacy. But no compassion, Sir—(*To Dawson*) We want leisure for't—This way.

[*Exeunt.*

487

SCENE II. changes to Beverley's lodgings.

Enter Mrs. Beverley, and Charlotte.

Mrs. Bev. No news of Lewson yet?

Char. None. He went out early, and knows not what has happened.

Mrs. Bev. The clock strikes eight—I'll wait no longer.

Char. Stay but till Jarvis comes. He has sent twice to stop us till we see him.

Mrs. Bev. I have no life in this separation. O! what a night was last night! I would not pass another such, to purchase worlds by it. My poor Beverley too! What must He have felt!—The very thought distracts me! To have him torn at midnight from me! A loathsome prison his habitation! A cold damp room his lodging! The bleak winds, perhaps, blowing upon his pillow! No fond wife to lull him to his rest! and no reflections but to wound and tear him!—'Tis too horrible! I wanted love for him, or they had not forced him from me. They should have parted soul and body first. I was too tame.

Char. You must not talk so. All that we could we did; and Jarvis did the rest. The faithful creature will give him comfort. Why does he delay coming?

Mrs. Bev. And there's another fear. His poor master may be claiming the last kind office from him—His heart perhaps is breaking.

Char. See where he comes!—His looks are chearful too.

488

SCENE III.

Enter Jarvis.

Mrs. Bev. Are tears then chearful? Alas, he weeps! Speak to him Charlotte: I have no tongue to ask him questions.

Char. How does your master, Jarvis?

Jar. I am old and foolish, madam; and tears will come before my words—But don't You weep. (*To Mrs. Beverley.*) I have a tale of joy for you.

Mrs. Bev. What tale? Say but he's well, and I have joy enough.

Jar. His mind too shall be well; all shalt be well—I have news for him that shall make his poor heart bound again!—Fie upon old age! how childish it makes me! I have a tale of joy for you, and my tears drown it.

Char. Shed them in showers then, and make haste to tell it.

Mrs. Bev. What is it, Jarvis?

Jar. Yet why should I rejoice when a good man dies? Your uncle, madam, died yesterday.

Mrs. Bev. My uncle!—O heavens!

Char. How heard you of his death?

Jar. His steward came express, madam: I met him in the street, enquiring for your lodgings. I should not rejoice, perhaps; but he was old, and my poor master a prisoner—Now he shall live again—O, 'tis a brave fortune! and 'twas death to me to see him a prisoner.

Char. Where left you the steward?

Jar. I would not bring him hither, to be a witness of your distresses—and besides, I wanted once before I die, to be the messenger of joy t'you. My good master will be a man again.

489Rrr

Mrs. Bev. Haste, haste then; and let us fly to him!—We are delaying our own happiness.

Jar. I had forgot a coach, madam; and Lucy has ordered one.

Mrs. Bev. Where was the need of that? The news has given me wings.

Char. I have no joy, till my poor brother shares it with me. How did he pass the night, Jarvis?

Jar. Why now, madam, I can tell you. Like a man dreaming of death and horrors. When they led him to his cell—for 'twas a poor apartment for my master—he flung himself upon a wretched bed, and lay speechless till day-break. A sigh now and then, and a few tears that followed those sighs, were all that told me he was alive. I spoke to him, but he would not hear me; and when I persisted, he raised his hand at me, and knit his brow so—I thought he would have struck me.

Mrs. Bev. O miserable! But what said he, Jarvis? Or was he silent all night?

Jar. At day-break he started from the bed, and looking wildly at me, asked who I was. I told him, and bid him be of comfort— Begone, old wretch, says he—I have sworn never to know comfort—My wife! my child! my sister! I have undone them all, and will know no comfort—Then letting go his hold, and falling upon his knees, he imprecated curses on himself.

Mrs. Bev. This is too horrible!—But you did not leave him so?

Char. No, I am sure he did not.

Jar. I had not the heart, madam. By degrees I brought him to himself. A shower of tears came to his relief; and then he called me his kindest friend, and begged forgiveness 490 of me like a child—I was a child too, when he begged forgiveness of me; my heart throbbed so, I could not speak to him. He turned from me for a minute or two, and suppressing a few bitter sighs, enquired after his wretched family—Wretched was his word, madam—Asked how you bore the misery of last night—If you had goodness enough to see him in prison—And then begged me to hasten to you. I told him he must be more himself first—He promised me he would; and, bating a few sullen intervals, he became composed and easy. And then I left him; but not without an attendant; a servant in the prison, whom I hired to wait upon him. 'Tis an hour since we parted: I was prevented in my haste, to be the messenger of joy t'you.

Mrs. Bev. What a tale is this?—But we have staid too long—A coach is needless.

Char. Hark! I hear one at the door.

Jar. And Lucy comes to tell us — We'll away this moment.

Mrs. Bev. To comfort him, or die with him.

[*Exeunt.*

SCENE IV. changes to Stukely's lodgings.

Enter Stukely, Bates, and Dawson.

Stu. Here's presumptive evidence at least: or if we want more, why, we must swear more. But all unwillingly: we gain credit by reluctance. I have told you how to proceed. Beverley must die. We hunt him in view now, and must not slacken in the chace. 'Tis either death for Him, or shame and punishment for Us. Think of that, and remember your instructions. You, Bates, must to the prison immediately: I would be there but a few minutes 491Qqq2 before you. And you, Dawson, must follow in a few minutes after. So here we divide — But answer me; are you resolved upon this business like men?

Bates. Like villains rather — But you may depend upon us.

Stu. Like what we are then — You make no answer, Dawson — Compassion, I suppose, has seized you.

Daw. No; I have disclaimed it. My answer is Bates's — You may depend upon me.

Stu. Consider the reward! Riches and security! I have sworn to divide with you to the last shilling. So here we separate, till we meet in prison. Remember your instructions, and be men.

[*Exeunt.*

SCENE V. changes to a prison.

Beverley is discovered sitting. After a short pause, he starts up, and comes forward.

Bev. Why, there's an end then. I have judged deliberately, and the result is death. How the self-murderer's account may stand, I know not. But this I know; the load of hateful life oppresses me too much. The horrors of my soul are more than I can bear—(*Offers to kneel*) Father of mercy!—I cannot pray—Despair has laid his iron hand upon me, and sealed me for perdition—Conscience! conscience! thy clamours are too loud—Here's that shall silence them. (*Takes a vial out of his pocket, and looks at it.*) Thou art most friendly to the miserable. Come then, thou cordial for sick minds! come to my heart! (*Drinks*) O, that the grave would bury memory as well as body! For if the soul sees and feels the sufferings of those dear ones it leaves behind, the EVERLASTING has no vengeance to torment 492 it deeper—I'll think no more on't—Reflection comes too late. Once there was a time for't—but now 'tis past—Who's there?

SCENE VI.

Enter Jarvis.

Jar. One that hoped to see you with better looks. Why do you turn so from me? I have brought comfort with me—And see who comes to give it welcome!

Bev. My wife and sister! Why, 'tis but one pang more then, and farewel world.

[*Aside.*

SCENE VII.

Enter Mrs. Beverley, and Charlotte.

Mrs. Bev. Where is he? (*Runs and embraces him*) O, I have him! I have him! And now they shall never part us more! I have news, love, to make you happy for ever—but don't look coldly on me.

Char. How is it, brother?

Mrs. Bev. Alas! he hears us not. Speak to me, love. I have no heart to see you thus.

Bev. Nor I to bear the sense of so much shame. This is a sad place.

Mrs. Bev. We come to take you from it; to tell you that the world goes well again; that providence has seen our sorrows, and sent the means to heal them—Your uncle died yesterday.

Bev. My uncle!—No, do not say so—O! I am sick at heart!

Mrs. Bev. Indeed!—I meant to bring you comfort.

493

Bev. Tell me he lives then—If you would give me comfort, tell me he lives.

Mrs. Bev. And if I did, I have no power to raise the dead. He died yesterday.

Bev. And I am heir to him?

Jar. To his whole estate, Sir—But bear it patiently.

Bev. Well, well—(*Pausing*) Why, fame says I am rich then?

Mrs. Bev. And truly so—Why do you look so wildly?

Bev. Do I? The news was unexpected. But has he left me all?

Jar. All, all, Sir—He could not leave it from you.

Bev. I'm sorry for it.

Char. Sorry! Why sorry?

Bev. Your uncle's dead, Charlotte.

Char. Peace be with his soul then. Is it so terrible that an old man should die?

Bev. He should have been immortal.

Mrs. Bev. Heaven knows I wished not for his death. 'Twas the will of providence that he should die. Why are you disturbed so?

Bev. Has death no terrors in it?

Mrs. Bev. Not an old man's death. Yet if it troubles you, I wish him living.

Bev. And I, with all my heart.

Char. Why, what's the matter?

Bev. Nothing. How heard you of his death?

Mrs. Bev. His steward came express. Would I had never known it!

Bev. Or had heard it one day sooner—For I have a tale to tell, shall turn you into stone; or if the power of speech, remain, you shall kneel down and curse me.

494

Mrs. Bev. Alas! what tale is this? And why are we to curse you? I'll bless you for ever.

Bev. No; I have deserved no blessings. The world holds not such another wretch. All this large fortune, this second bounty of heaven, that might have healed our sorrows, and satisfied our utmost hopes, in a curst hour I sold last night.

Char. Sold! How sold?

Mrs. Bev. Impossible! It cannot be!

Bev. That devil Stukely, with all hell to aid him, tempted me to the deed. To pay false debts of honour, and to redeem past errors, I sold the reversion—sold it for a scanty sum, and lost it among villains.

Char. Why, farewel all then.

Bev. Liberty and life. Come, kneel and curse me.

Mrs. Bev. Then hear me heaven! (*Kneels*) Look down with mercy on his sorrows! Give softness to his looks, and quiet to his heart! Take from his memory the sense of what is past, and cure him of despair! On Me, on Me, if misery must be the lot of either, multiply misfortunes! I'll bear them patiently, so He is happy! These hands shall toil for his support! These eyes be lifted up for hourly blessings on him! And every duty of a fond and faithful wife, be doubly done to chear and comfort him!—So hear me! so reward me!

[*Rises.*

Bev. I would kneel too, but that offended heaven would turn my prayers to curses. What have I to ask for? I, who have shook hands with hope? Is it for length of days that I should kneel? No; My time is limited. Or is it for this world's blessings upon You and Yours? To pour out my heart in wishes for a ruined wife, a child and sister? O! no! For I have done a deed to make you miserable.

Mrs. Bev. Why miserable? Is poverty so miserable?—The real wants of life are few: a little industry will supply them all; and chearfulness will follow. It is the privilege of honest industry; and we'll enjoy it fully.

Bev. Never, never! O, I have told you but in part. The irrevocable deed is done.

Mrs. Bev. What deed? And why do you look so at me?

Bev. A deed, that dooms my soul to vengeance; that seals Your misery here, and Mine hereafter.

Mrs. Bev. No, no; You have a heart too good for't— Alas! he raves, Charlotte—his looks too terrify me—Speak comfort to him—He can have done no deed of wickedness.

Char. And yet I fear the worst. What is it, brother?

Bev. A deed of horror.

Jar. Ask him no questions, madam. This last misfortune has hurt his brain. A little time will give him patience.

SCENE VIII.

Enter Stukely.

Bev. Why is this villain here?

Stu. To give You liberty and safety. There's his discharge, madam. (*Giving a paper to Mrs. Beverley*) Let him begone this moment. The arrest last night was meant in friendship; but came too late.

Char. What mean you, Sir?

Stu. The arrest was too late, I say. I would have kept his hands from blood, but was too late.

Mrs. Bev. His hands from blood! Whose blood?—O, wretch! wretch!

Stu. From Lewson's blood.

Char. No, villain! Yet what of Lewson? Speak quickly!

Stu. You are ignorant then! I thought I heard the murderer at confession.

Char. What murderer? And who is murdered? Not Lewson? Say he lives, and I'll kneel down and worship you.

Stu. In pity, so I would; but that the tongues of all cry murder. I came in pity, not in malice; to save the brother, not kill the sister. Your Lewson's dead.

Char. O horrible! Why, who has killed him?—And yet it cannot be. What crime had He committed that he should die? Villain! he lives! he lives! and shall revenge these pangs.

Mrs. Bev. Patience, sweet Charlotte!

Char. O, 'tis too much for patience!

Mrs. Bev. He comes in pity, he says. O! execrable villain! The friend is killed then, and this the murderer?

Bev. Silence, I charge you. Proceed, Sir.

Stu. No. Justice may stop the tale—and here's an evidence.

SCENE IX.

Enter Bates.

Bates. The news, I see, has reached you. But take comfort, madam. (*To Charlotte*) There's one without, enquiring for you. Go to him, and lose no time.

Char. O misery! misery!

[*Exit.*

Mrs. Bev. Follow her, Jarvis. If it be true that Lewson's dead, her grief may kill her.

Bates. Jarvis must stay here, madam: I have some questions for him.

Stu. Rather let him fly. His evidence may crush his master.

497Sss

Bev. Why, ay; this looks like management.

Bates. He found you quarrelling with Lewson in the street last night.

[*To Beverley.*

Mrs. Bev. No; I am sure he did not.

Jar. Or if I did—

Mrs. Bev. 'Tis false, old man—They had no quarrel; there was no cause for quarrel.

Bev. Let him proceed, I say—O! I am sick! sick! Reach me a chair.

[*He sits down.*

Mrs. Bev. You droop, and tremble, love—Your eyes are fixt too—Yet You are innocent. If Lewson's dead, You killed him not.

SCENE X.

Enter Dawson.

Stu. Who sent for Dawson?

Bates. 'Twas I. We have a witness too, you little think of. Without there!

Stu. What witness?

Bates. A right one. Look at him.

SCENE XI.

Re-enter Charlotte, with Lewson.

Stu. Lewson! O—villains! villains!

[*To Bates and Dawson.*

Mrs. Bev. Risen from the dead! Why, this is unexpected happiness!

Char. Or is't his ghost? (*To Stukely*) That sight would please you, Sir.

Jar. What riddle's this?

Bev. Be quick and tell it—My minutes are but few.

498

Mrs. Bev. Alas! why so? You shall live long and happily.

Lew. While shame and punishment shall rack that viper. (*Pointing to Stukely*) The tale is short. I was too busy in his secrets, and therefore doomed to die. Bates, to prevent the murder, undertook it. I kept aloof to give it credit —

Char. And gave Me pangs unutterable.

Lew. I felt them all, and would have told you; but vengeance wanted ripening. The villain's scheme was but half executed. The arrest by Dawson followed the supposed murder: and now, depending on his once wicked associates, he comes to fix the guilt on Beverley.

Mrs. Bev. O! execrable wretch!

Bates. Dawson and I are witnesses of this.

Lew. And of a thousand frauds. His friend undone by sharpers and false dice; and Stukely sole contriver, and possessor of all.

Daw. Had he but stopt on this side murder, we had been villains still.

Mrs. Bev. Thus heaven turns evil into good; and by permitting sin, warns men to virtue.

Lew. Yet punishes the instrument. So shall our laws; though not with death. But death were mercy. Shame, beggary, and imprisonment, unpitied misery, the stings of conscience, and the curses of mankind shall make life hateful to him — till at last, his own hand end him. How does my friend?

[*To Beverley.*

Bev. Why, well. Who's he that asks me?

Mrs. Bev. Tis Lewson, love. Why do you look so at him?

Bev. They told me he was murdered.

[*Wildly.*

Mrs. Bev. Ay; but he lives to save us.

Bev. Lend me your hand — The room turns round.

499Sss2

Mrs. Bev. O heaven!

Lew. This villain here, disturbs him. Remove him from his sight: and for your lives, see that you guard him. (*Stukely is taken off by Dawson and Bates*) How is it, Sir?

Bev. 'Tis here—and here—(*Pointing to his head and heart.*) And now it tears me!

Mrs. Bev. You feel convulsed too—What is't disturbs you?

Lew. This sudden turn of joy perhaps. He wants rest too. Last night was dreadful to him. His brain is giddy.

Char. Ay, never to be cured. Why, brother!—O! I fear! I fear!

Mrs. Bev. Preserve him, heaven!—My love! my life! look at me!— How his eyes flame!

Bev. A furnace rages in this heart—I have been too hasty.

Mrs. Bev. Indeed!—O me! O me!—Help, Jarvis! Fly, fly for help! Your master dies else—Weep not, but fly! (*Exit Jarvis*) What is this hasty deed?—Yet do not answer me—My fears have guessed it.

Bev. Call back the messenger. 'Tis not in medicine's power to help me.

Mrs. Bev. Is it then so?

Bev. Down, restless flames!—(*Laying his hand on his heart*) down to your native hell!— there you shall rack me—O! for a pause from pain!

Mrs. Bev. Help, Charlotte! Support him, Sir! (*To Lewson*)

Bev. What river's this? I'll plunge, and cool me! (*Flings himself upon the ground.*) O! 'tis a sea of fire!—Lift me! lift me!

[*They raise him to his chair.*

Mrs. Bev. This is a killing fight!

Bev. (*Starting*) That pang was well. It has numbed my senses. Where's my wife? Can you forgive me, love?

500

Mrs. Bev. Alas! for what?

Bev. (Starting again) And there's another pang—Now all is quiet. Will you forgive me?

Mrs. Bev. I will. Tell me for what?

Bev. For meanly dying.

Mrs. Bev. No—do not say it.

Bev. As truly as my soul must answer it. Had Jarvis staid this morning, all had been well. But pressed by shame; pent in a prison; tormented with my pangs for You; driven to despair and madness; I took the advantage of his absence, corrupted the poor wretch he left to guard me, and—swallowed poison.

Mrs. Bev. O! fatal deed!

Char. Dreadful and cruel!

Bev. Ay, most accursed—And now I go to my account. This rest from pain brings death; yet 'tis heaven's kindness to me. I wished for ease, a moment's ease, that cool repentance and contrition might soften vengeance. Bend me, and let me kneel. (*They lift him from his chair, and support him on his knees*) I'll pray for You too. Thou Power that mad'st me, hear me! If for a life of frailty, and this too hasty deed of death, thy justice dooms me, here I acquit the sentence. But if, enthroned in mercy where thou sitt'st, thy pity has beheld me, send me a gleam of hope; that in these last and bitter moments, my soul may taste of comfort! And for these mourners here, O! let their lives be peaceful, and their deaths happy! Now raise me.

[*They lift him to the chair.*

Mrs. Bev. Restore him, heaven! Stretch forth thy arm omnipotent, and snatch him from the grave! O save him! save him!

Bev. Alas! that prayer is fruitless: already death has seized me. Yet heaven is gracious. I asked for hope, as the 501 bright presage of forgiveness, and like a light, blazing through darkness, it came and cheared me. 'Twas all I lived for, and now I die.

Mrs. Bev. Not yet!—Not yet!—Stay but a little, and I'll die too.

Bev. No; live, I charge you. We have a little one: though I have left him, You will not leave him. To Lewson's kindness I bequeath him — Is not this Charlotte? We have lived in love, though I have wronged you — Can you forgive me, Charlotte?

Char. Forgive you! — O, my poor brother!

Bev. Lend me your hand, love. So — raise me — No — 'twill not be — my life is finished — O! for a few short moments to tell you how my heart bleeds for you! — That even now, thus dying as I am, dubious and fearful of hereafter, my bosom pang is for Your miseries! — Support her heaven! — And now I go — O, mercy! mercy!

[*Dies.*

Lew. Then all is over — How is it, madam? (*To Mrs. Beverley.*) My poor Charlotte too!

SCENE the last.

Enter Jarvis.

Jar. How does my master, madam? Here's help at hand — Am I too late then?

[*Seeing Beverley.*

Char. Tears! tears! why fall you not? O wretched sister! — Speak to her, Lewson — her grief is speechless.

Lew. Remove her from this sight. Go to her, Jarvis; lead and support her. Sorrow like hers forbids complaint. Words are for lighter griefs. Some ministring angel bring her peace! (*Jarvis and Charlotte lead her off.*) And Thou, 502 poor breathless corps, may thy departed soul have found the rest it prayed for! Save but one error, and this last fatal deed, thy life was lovely. Let frailer minds take warning; and from example learn, that want of prudence is want of virtue.

Follies, if uncontroul'd, of every kind,
Grow into passions, and subdue the mind;
With sense and reason hold superior strife,
And conquer honour, nature, fame and life.

503

94

EPILOGUE.

Written by a FRIEND,

And Spoken by Mrs. PRITCHARD.

On every GAMESTER *in th' Arabian nation,*
'Tis said, that Mahomet denounc'd damnation;
But in return for wicked cards and dice,
He gave them black-ey'd girls in paradise.
Should he thus preach, good countrymen, to You,
His converts would, I fear, be mighty few:
So much your hearts are set on sordid gain,
The brightest eyes around you shine in vain:
Should the most heav'nly beauty bid you take her,
You'd rather hold – two aces and a maker.
By your example, our poor sex drawn in,
Is guilty of the same unnat'ral sin:
The study now of every girl of parts
Is how to win your money, not your hearts.
O! in what sweet, what ravishing delights,
Our beaux and belles together pass their nights!
By ardent perturbations kept awake,
Each views with longing eyes the other's – stake.
504 The smiles and graces are from Britain flown,
Our Cupid *is an errant sharper grown,*
And Fortune *sits on* Cytherea's *throne.*
In all these things, though women may be blam'd,
Sure men, the wiser men, should be asham'd!
And 'tis a horrid scandal, I declare,
That four strange queens should rival all the fair;
Four jilts, with neither beauty, wit nor parts,
O shame! have got possession of their hearts;
And those bold sluts, for all their queenly pride,
Have play'd loose tricks, or else they're much bely'd.
Cards were at first for benefits design'd,
Sent to amuse, and not enslave the mind:
From good to bad how easy the transition!
For what was pleasure once, is now perdition.

Fair ladies, then these GAMESTERS shun,
Whoever weds one, is, you see, undone.

FINIS.

*Act 5.*THE GAMESTER.*Sc. 4.*

Mr. REDDISH as BEVERLEY.

Bev.— Thou art most friendly to the miserable.

MR. REDDISH as BEVERLEY.

Bev. – *Thou art most friendly to the miserable.*

Published Octo. 19, 1776, by T. Lowndes & Partners

THE AUGUSTAN REPRINT SOCIETY

ANNOUNCES ITS

Publications for the Third Year (1948-1949)

[Transcriber's Note:
Many of the listed titles are or will be available from Project Gutenberg. Where possible, a link to the e-text is given.]

At least two items will be printed from each of the *three* following groups:

Men, Manners, and Critics
Sir John Falstaff (pseud.), *The Theatre* (1720).
Series IV: Aaron Hill, Preface to *The Creation*; and Thomas Brereton, Preface to *Esther*.
Ned Ward, Selected Tracts.

Drama
Edward Moore, *The Gamester* (1753).
Series V: Nevil Payne, *Fatal Jealousy* (1673).
Mrs. Centlivre, *The Busie Body* (1709).
Charles Macklin, *Man of the World* (1781).

Poetry and Language
John Oldmixon, *Reflections on Dr. Swift's Letter to Harley*
Series VI: (1712); and Arthur Mainwaring, *The British Academy* (1712).
Pierre Nicole, *De Epigrammate.*

Andre Dacier, Essay on Lyric Poetry.

THE AUGUSTAN REPRINT SOCIETY

MAKES AVAILABLE

Inexpensive Reprints of Rare Materials

FROM

ENGLISH LITERATURE OF THE
SEVENTEENTH AND EIGHTEENTH CENTURIES

Students, scholars, and bibliographers of literature, history, and philology will find the publications valuable. *The Johnsonian News Letter* has said of them: "Excellent facsimiles, and cheap in price, these represent the triumph of modern scientific reproduction. Be sure to become a subscriber; and take it upon yourself to see that your college library is on the mailing list."

The Augustan Reprint Society is a non-profit, scholarly organization, run without overhead expense. By careful management it is able to offer at least six publications each year at the unusually low membership fee of $2.50 per year in the United States and Canada, and $2.75 in Great Britain and the continent.

Libraries as well as individuals are eligible for membership. Since the publications are issued without profit, however, no discount can be allowed to libraries, agents, or booksellers.

New members may still obtain a complete run of the first year's publications for $2.50, the annual membership fee.

During the first two years the publications are issued in three series: I. Essays on Wit; II. Essays on Poetry and Language; and III. Essays on the Stage.

PUBLICATIONS FOR THE FIRST YEAR (1946-1947)

MAY, 1946:
Series I, No. 1—Richard Blackmore's *Essay upon Wit* (1716), and Addison's *Freeholder* No. 45 (1716).

JULY, 1946:
Series II, No. 1—Samuel Cobb's *Of Poetry* and *Discourse on Criticism* (1707)

SEPT., 1946:
Series III, No. 1—Anon., *Letter to A.H. Esq.; concerning the Stage* (1698), and Richard Willis' *Occasional Paper* No. IX (1698).

NOV., 1946:
Series I, No. 2—Anon., *Essay on Wit* (1748), together with Characters by Flecknoe, and Joseph Warton's *Adventurer* Nos. 127 and 133.

JAN., 1947:
Series II, No. 2—Samuel Wesley's *Epistle to a Friend Concerning Poetry* (1700) and *Essay on Heroic Poetry* (1693).

MARCH, 1947:
Series III, No. 2—Anon., *Representation of the Impiety and Immorality of the Stage* (1704) and anon., *Some Thoughts Concerning the Stage* (1704).

PUBLICATIONS FOR THE SECOND YEAR (1947-1948)

MAY, 1947:
Series I, No. 3—John Gay's *The Present State of Wit;* and a section on Wit from *The English Theophrastus.* With an Introduction by Donald Bond.

JULY, 1947:
Series II, No. 3—Rapin's *De Carmine Pastorali,* translated by Creech. With an Introduction by J. E.

Congleton.

SEPT., 1947:	Series III, No. 3—T. Hanmer's (?) *Some Remarks on the Tragedy of Hamlet*. With an Introduction by Clarence D. Thorpe.
NOV., 1947:	Series I, No. 4—Corbyn Morris' *Essay towards Fixing the True Standards of Wit,* etc. With an Introduction by James L. Clifford.
JAN., 1948:	Series II, No. 4—Thomas Purney's *Discourse on the Pastoral*. With an Introduction by Earl Wasserman.
MARCH, 1948:	Series III, No. 4—Essays on the Stage, selected, with an Introduction by Joseph Wood Krutch.

The list of publications is subject to modification in response to requests by members. From time to time Bibliographical Notes will be included in the issues. Each issue contains an Introduction by a scholar of special competence in the field represented.

The Augustan Reprints are available only to members. They will never be offered at "remainder" prices.

GENERAL EDITORS

RICHARD C. BOYS, *University of Michigan*
EDWARD NILES HOOKER, *University of California, Los Angeles*
H. T. SWEDENBERG, JR., *University of California, Los Angeles*

ADVISORY EDITORS

EMMETT L. AVERY, *State College of Washington*
LOUIS I. BREDVOLD, *University of Michigan*
BENJAMIN BOYCE, *University of Nebraska*
CLEANTH BROOKS, *Louisiana State University*